W9-AVY-030

"This is beginning to sound worse and worse."

Ben shook his head and ran his fingers through his hair.

"Ben—" she said.

"Let me finish," he said, holding up his hand, "before I change my mind. Hank's been parading women in front of me for years, hoping I'd be interested in one. Funny, I wasn't even suspicious about you—not in that way. I thought you were after him—the old lech."

"I'm not responsible for Hank's manipulations."

Ben held up his hand again. "I know that. That's not why I stayed away this week. I had to sort out my feelings. My trip to Arizona was . . . convenient."

Tonia held her breath, not knowing whether to hug or slug the man she loved. "And did you sort out your feelings?" she asked.

He shrugged. "No."

Tonia lifted her hands palm upward and let them drop into her lap. "Then why are you here?"

American author **Patricia Knoll** lives in California with her husband, a technical editor, and their family of five, four sons and a daughter. She had been a "closet writer" for years, but only began mailing out short stories and books in 1981 after the birth of baby number four. She sold her first two books in 1984 and 1985; *Gypsy Enchantment* is her first book in the Harlequin Romance line. Growing up in a western copper-mining town, she has always been fascinated by people and the stories they had to tell. Now she enjoys creating the worlds they live in and giving them a happy ending.

Gypsy Enchantment

Patricia Knoll

Harlequin Books

TORONTO • NEW YORK • LONDON
AMSTERDAM • PARIS • SYDNEY • HAMBURG
STOCKHOLM • ATHENS • TOKYO • MILAN

ISBN 0-373-02902-0

Harlequin Romance first edition April 1988

This book is dedicated to
Andy, Adam, Joanna, and Alex.
Kids, this is what I've been doing
when you couldn't get my attention.

Copyright © 1988 Patricia Knoll.
Philippine copyright 1988. Australian copyright 1988.
All rights reserved. Except for use in any review, the reproduction or utilization
of this work in whole or in part in any form by any electronic, mechanical
or other means, now known or hereafter invented, including xerography,
photocopying and recording, or in any information storage or retrieval system,
is forbidden without the permission of the publisher, Harlequin Enterprises
Limited, 225 Duncan Mill Road, Don Mills, Ontario, Canada M3B 3K9. All the
characters in this book have no existence outside the imagination of the
author and have no relation whatsoever to anyone bearing the same name
or names. They are not even distantly inspired by any individual known
or unknown to the author, and all incidents are pure invention.

The Harlequin trademarks, consisting of the words HARLEQUIN ROMANCE
and the portrayal of a Harlequin, are trademarks of Harlequin Enterprises
Limited; the portrayal of a Harlequin is registered in the United States Patent
and Trademark Office and in the Canada Trade Marks Office.

Printed in U.S.A.

CHAPTER ONE

TONIA LEANED BACK on her hands and dug her fingers into the sand. Back arched, she lifted her face to the sun and raised her knees. Scarlet-tipped toenails disappeared in the sand as she flexed her feet against the grainy texture. There was something very soothing about feeling the earth beneath one's feet.

She sighed and let the day's tensions ease out of the knotted muscles at the back of her neck. Hours of squinting at tiny print in dusty old books and yellowed newspapers were a strain, and for an instant she longed to wander the world with her Gypsy relatives, enjoying each day as much as she was enjoying this moment.

The raucous cries of two squabbling seagulls brought her back to reality. The scavenging birds patrolled this stretch of beach daily and Tonia had quickly learned to save part of her lunch to throw them as she approached, or risk being dive-bombed.

The pair reminded her of the old comedy team, Abbott and Costello: fighting constantly but always together. They battled over every scrap of food and when it was gone, they fought about that.

Costello, the plump one, seemed to think she was his special property. When he had finished the remnants of her lunch, he would hop toward her, too wary to come close, but too gluttonous to let her escape without giving him more food. He began his dancing approach as she watched, amused by his unappealing shape and blatant greed.

"I can't let you marry him, you know."

For a wild instant, Tonia thought the husky male voice, raised over the sound of the surf, was speaking to her *and* Costello. Without being too obvious, she looked out of the corner of her eye to see who he *was* talking to.

"You are Antonia Meier, aren't you?"

Tonia turned her head to look up at a man who was tall, good-looking and extremely irritated.

At this intrusion in their territory, the gulls took off in startled flight and circled for a moment to see if the man might have food to throw them. When he remained unmoving, staring at Tonia, they soared away.

Viewing the man's grim face, Tonia decided she had better do the same. Her hand snaked out to snag her keys and the high-heeled sandals she had discarded. She sloughed her feet around beneath her and rose, her eyes never leaving his face.

His gaze traveled from her bare feet, to her loosely belted red and yellow print dress and chunky gold necklace to finally stop at her face.

In her bright dress, with her blue-black hair whipping about wildly, she looked untamed. The expression around his mouth told Tonia he didn't like what he saw, and she felt that she was literally caught between the devil and the deep blue sea.

"Yes, I'm Antonia Meier."

"I'm Ben Andrews. Benjamin *Tyson* Andrews."

The tautness eased from her body and she smiled. "You're a relative of Hank Tyson's?"

He didn't answer immediately, but dug his hands into the pockets of his pleated linen slacks and tilted his head to one side. The ocean breeze flirted with his ash-brown hair, toss-

Caught up in his own thoughts, he ignored her defense of Hank's new housekeeper. "He's writing a book—" Ben spread his hands wide and looked heavenward "—a *book* for crying out loud!"

Tonia frowned. "What's adolescent about that?"

"Well, nothing in itself. But this is a man who thinks that if God had meant us to write letters He would have given us pens instead of fingers." Ben took a deep breath and continued with his list of grievances. "He's picked up a research assistant who—" He stopped, his face flushing a dull red.

"Yes," Tonia said. "What about me?"

He studied her for an instant before thrusting his chin out and continuing defiantly. "A research assistant who's too sexy to do what Hank says she can do. I have to admit that when I first saw you I thought Hank's hormones had staged a coup d'état on his brain!"

Tonia's lips pursed at the chauvinistic remark. Again she retrieved her sandals and keys and started walking down the beach to Hank's house.

Ben fell into step beside her. "He says he wants to marry you."

"I can't help what he says."

"It's true then," Ben pounced.

"No, it isn't!"

"Well, how do you explain . . . ?"

Tonia's steps quickened, but with his longer legs he strode along easily, while she almost ran. She thought they must look pretty strange, stomping down the beach, glaring at each other. "I told you, Mr. Andrews, it's a joke."

"I wish I could believe that."

"Believe it!" Tonia snapped. "I'm qualified to do the job for which your uncle hired me. I'm sorry if the changes in him are a shock, but they have nothing to do with me. I'm his employee. Nothing more. There hasn't been a hint of anything romantic between us. What, exactly, did Hank say?''

"That he loved Tonia Meier, and was even thinking of marriage.''

Tonia shook her head. "I'll bet I can tell you exactly how he said it, too. His eyes were sparkling, and he was rubbing his hands together, wasn't he?''

"Well, yes.''

"Hook, line and sinker," Tonia said. "Don't worry about it, I fell for the first few jokes he played on me, too. It's hard to believe that someone with such a sweet face could be such a stinker.''

They had reached the high seawall that kept the Pacific Ocean out of Hank's backyard. Tonia walked to the gate that locked automatically when someone exited. Unlocking it with the key Hank had given her, she pushed it open and ran up the back steps. Ben was right behind her as she dusted off her feet, slipped on her sandals and hurried into the kitchen.

"Miss Meier, listen." His conciliatory tone stopped her at the entrance to the dining room. Ben took his glasses out of his pocket and slipped them on his nose. "You're right. This probably has nothing to do with you, really. It's Hank's problem. Maybe I should call his doctor....''

Tonia pushed open the swinging door to the dining room with its elegant, antique cherry wood table and exquisite hand-carved chairs. Ben followed, muttering under his breath. "Maybe it's a second childhood....''

"Talk to Hank about it," she advised. "There's probably a perfectly reasonable explanation.''

Next to the dining room was the small den she shared with Hank during working hours. She got her purse from her desk and headed toward the front door. A clatter of footsteps on the staircase stopped her. She glanced up to see her new employer coming down.

Dressed in beach sandals, cutoffs, and an eye-watering Hawaiian print shirt, Hank Tyson looked anything but his sixty-five years. One glance at his face told Tonia her guess had been right. He had been spying on them from his bedroom.

He all but tap-danced down the steps and across the parquet floor to join them. Warily, Tonia assessed the devilish light gleaming in his blue eyes, and glanced at Ben, who had resumed his frown.

Hank stopped and favored them with a big grin. "There she is," he cried. "The girl who's stolen my heart away!"

Ben's frost-gray eyes met hers. "A perfectly reasonable explanation, hmm?"

Tonia's answering smile was feeble as she backed toward the door.

THE FOURTEEN-YEAR-OLD Volkswagen jerked, voicing its protest, belching exhaust and smoke into the air as Tonia slowed for a red light. She wanted to avoid shifting into first. Once she had the car going, she tried to miss red lights and stop signs.

Teeth worrying her bottom lip, she thought about Ben's concern. Hank's last remark had been pretty strange, she admitted. But, then, the entire circumstances of her hiring had been pretty strange.

Dr. Justin, her anthropology professor at the university had called to say a Mr. Henry Tyson wanted to write a book and needed a research assistant. Would Tonia be interested? Bored with her secretarial job at an aerospace firm, Tonia had said yes immediately.

When she had called Mr. Tyson, he had sounded delighted, and promised to come right over and interview her—at her house!

The red light changed and Tonia drove through the intersection, smiling at the memory of the peppery little man who had bounced up to her front door and stayed until she'd invited him to share her dinner.

"You're a fine cook, young lady," he'd said as he helped himself to more shrimp salad. "Pretty, too. Yes sir, I think you'll be a great addition to the household."

"Well, I hope I'll be more than decorative, Mr. Tyson," she'd answered dryly, watching him wolf down the salad she had planned to have in her lunches all week. "You'll probably want to review my references."

"Not necessary." He waved off her suggestion. "Dr. Justin's recommendation is good enough for me. He says he even knows a student who can keep house for me."

Tonia pounced on the mention of the professor. "Have you known Dr. Justin long?" Hank Tyson didn't seem like the type to be a friend of the professor, who delighted in surrounding himself with bright young students.

"Never met him. Someone recommended I call him, said he might know a secretary interested in working for me."

"Oh, who told you to call, Mr. Tyson?"

"Don't remember right now. Are you going to eat that last roll? And call me Hank!"

After dinner, he'd prowled her living and dining rooms with a cup of coffee in his hand, studying the decor. She and her mother tended to favor bright colors. The rooms were done in shades of turquoise, yellow and red, toned down with dark-stained oak furnishings. Pictures of her family were displayed on the walls or in frames on the bookcase. Hank's attention was captured for several minutes by a photo of six-year-old Tonia riding on her father's shoul-

When she had called Mr. Tyson, he had sounded delighted, and promised to come right over and interview her—at her house!

The red light changed and Tonia drove through the intersection, smiling at the memory of the peppery little man who had bounced up to her front door and stayed until she'd invited him to share her dinner.

"You're a fine cook, young lady," he'd said as he helped himself to more shrimp salad. "Pretty, too. Yes sir, I think you'll be a great addition to the household."

"Well, I hope I'll be more than decorative, Mr. Tyson," she'd answered dryly, watching him wolf down the salad she had planned to have in her lunches all week. "You'll probably want to review my references."

"Not necessary." He waved off her suggestion. "Dr. Justin's recommendation is good enough for me. He says he even knows a student who can keep house for me."

Tonia pounced on the mention of the professor. "Have you known Dr. Justin long?" Hank Tyson didn't seem like the type to be a friend of the professor, who delighted in surrounding himself with bright young students.

"Never met him. Someone recommended I call him, said he might know a secretary interested in working for me."

"Oh, who told you to call, Mr. Tyson?"

"Don't remember right now. Are you going to eat that last roll? And call me Hank!"

After dinner, he'd prowled her living and dining rooms with a cup of coffee in his hand, studying the decor. She and her mother tended to favor bright colors. The rooms were done in shades of turquoise, yellow and red, toned down with dark-stained oak furnishings. Pictures of her family were displayed on the walls or in frames on the bookcase. Hank's attention was captured for several minutes by a photo of six-year-old Tonia riding on her father's shoul-

steps on the staircase stopped her. She glanced up to see her new employer coming down.

Dressed in beach sandals, cutoffs, and an eye-watering Hawaiian print shirt, Hank Tyson looked anything but his sixty-five years. One glance at his face told Tonia her guess had been right. He had been spying on them from his bedroom.

He all but tap-danced down the steps and across the parquet floor to join them. Warily, Tonia assessed the devilish light gleaming in his blue eyes, and glanced at Ben, who had resumed his frown.

Hank stopped and favored them with a big grin. "There she is," he cried. "The girl who's stolen my heart away!"

Ben's frost-gray eyes met hers. "A perfectly reasonable explanation, hmm?"

Tonia's answering smile was feeble as she backed toward the door.

THE FOURTEEN-YEAR-OLD Volkswagen jerked, voicing its protest, belching exhaust and smoke into the air as Tonia slowed for a red light. She wanted to avoid shifting into first. Once she had the car going, she tried to miss red lights and stop signs.

Teeth worrying her bottom lip, she thought about Ben's concern. Hank's last remark had been pretty strange, she admitted. But, then, the entire circumstances of her hiring had been pretty strange.

Dr. Justin, her anthropology professor at the university had called to say a Mr. Henry Tyson wanted to write a book and needed a research assistant. Would Tonia be interested? Bored with her secretarial job at an aerospace firm, Tonia had said yes immediately.

in a rough-edged way. Energy and purpose seemed to simmer in his eyes.

She was pleased to see him.

Tonia threw her head back and smiled up into Ben's face. "Good morning." When he grinned, her heart seemed to jump right up into her throat and stick there. She was blocking the door, but for the life of her, she couldn't think of a single reason to move away.

BEN WONDERED if she had any idea how lovely she looked, with her coal-black hair swirling around her shoulders, face flushed, ebony eyes sparkling, minty breath puffing out in tiny gasps as though she had been running. In spite of his confusion and irritation the day before, he couldn't help noticing her exotic looks.

Her dark eyes had a mysterious up-slant at the corners, giving her a look of secret humor even when she wasn't smiling. Her full lips had a near pout to them that was very appealing. She wore a lightweight sweater and skirt of eye-popping pink that leant a creaminess to her olive complexion. Several strands of hair had been blown across her face to tangle with her eyelashes.

He lifted a hand and brushed the midnight strands away from her face and curled some of the silky stuff around his fingers. What was that elusive scent she wore, he wondered, some kind of flower? Jasmine? No, honeysuckle, he decided triumphantly. Funny, he would have thought she'd wear a more exotic scent. Opium, perhaps. Or Shalimar. He drew the strands of hair toward his face, intent on touching them to his lips.

Tonia blinked at Ben's intent expression. For the length of a heartbeat, she seemed to sway toward him. Then, as if flustered by his touch, she stepped back. "I'm—I'm sorry, Mr. Andrews. I didn't mean to block the door."

Ben glanced down at his hands, wondering if they'd developed a mind of their own, and stuffed them into his pockets. He pulled them out again, took his glasses out of his suit jacket and put them on. "Call me Ben, Tonia," he said, blinking at her through the lenses. "I think we're going to be seeing a lot of each other."

"Oh, probably." She laughed breathlessly. "Do you live here? I thought Hank lived alone."

"No, I have an apartment in La Jolla. Sometimes I sleep over here when Hank and I get involved in a poker game with some of his cronies. Every once in a while he gets it into his head that he can beat me."

"Hah," the older man grumbled from the door to the living room. "I could, too, if you didn't cheat. I thought I'd raised you to play fair. One of these days I'm going to figure out how you do it."

Ben chuckled at the deep affection that ran between the two men, and Tonia smiled.

"Come have some coffee, Tonia, before we start work," Hank said. "You look like you could use some."

"I could," she admitted, flashing Ben another smile before moving into the hallway.

"I'll join you as soon as I put this in the car." Ben lifted his black leather briefcase.

"I thought you said you had to get to your office." Hank's gray brows were pulled together in a frown over his shrewd blue eyes.

"I changed my mind." Ben shrugged. He headed down the steps and out toward a silver sports car parked on the street.

He unsnapped one corner of the vinyl cover that protected the interior of his Lotus Super Seven. He'd been nervous about leaving it parked on the street all night. He wouldn't have done it if he hadn't been so worried about

Hank. The space usually reserved for him in Hank's two-car garage had been taken up with a sporty new compact. Under Ben's relentless questioning, Hank had admitted that he'd bought it on a lark, defending his actions by pointing out how many sporty cars Ben owned. Mystified, Ben had looked from the new car to Hank's staid older sedan, shaking his head. Hank had watched him, chortling.

Ben glanced at his watch. He should be on his way to the office now. Plans for the opening of his newest auto-parts store in Chula Vista were coming together, and his desk would be groaning under the weight of several weeks' work awaiting his attention. He *should* go, but he wanted to see Hank and his assistant together.

He was wary of Tonia. For a moment in the hallway he had felt dazed, inexplicably drawn to her. He couldn't remember ever feeling such an instant attraction to a woman. He didn't think Tonia was even aware of it.

He shifted uncomfortably. She might be having the same effect on Hank.

Ben slipped the briefcase under the vinyl cover and snapped it down again, then automatically checked the Seven's silver surface for any spots of tarnish. He reached under the cover again, pulled out a soft rag, and gave the hood a few careful wipes.

After spending the evening and most of the night playing poker with Hank and two of his friends, he should feel reassured, he thought. Hank had acted pretty normal, except for the loud pink Hawaiian shirt he had worn. Antonia Meier was probably right; Hank's vacation had just done more good than he had expected. Ben scowled. He just hoped Hank didn't make a damned fool of himself.

Still deep in thought, Ben went back up the walk and eased the front door open. Tonia was on the phone, her back to him, her long black hair falling forward, hiding her

face. As he started to walk past quietly, her words stopped
him.

"A new one!" she snorted into the receiver. "Fat chance!
I guess it's time to bury him. I probably just wore him out.
Poor Ralph."

Ralph? Who the hell was Ralph?

"I wish he'd gone in an accident," Tonia rushed on,
twining the phone cord around her fingers. "Then at least
I could get some insurance money. This way I don't get
anything!"

Insurance money?

"Yes, I know he was old..."

How old?

Tonia sighed. "Thanks for calling, Paul, and thanks for
the sympathy."

Tonia hung up, turning slowly away from the phone table and hooking her dangling earring back into place. Ben
peeled his hand off the knob and pushed hard against the
door, slamming it.

CHAPTER TWO

TONIA STARTED. "Something wrong?"

Ben wore a piercing expression that he seemed to be struggling to control. "No, of course not. Shall we join Hank?"

She nodded doubtfully, thinking of the searching look he had given her earlier. This was different, unpleasant. Involuntarily, she shivered, then turned to precede him into the airy living room. No fog obscured the view of the beach, and the sun sparkled playfully on the surf. A few joggers loped down the sand in steady rhythm.

Personally she avoided exercise, reasoning that there should be at least one person left in the county who didn't sweat in public.

"Will you pour, Tonia?" Hank asked, pulling her attention back inside the room. Morning coffee had become a ritual with them.

Tonia sat on the plush brown velvet sofa and served coffee in Wedgwood cups that must have been a treasure of Hank's English wife, Maggie.

She handed cups to Hank and Ben, who had taken chairs opposite her. While the two men sipped their coffee, Tonia's gaze wandered around the room. Though large, it was sparsely furnished, with Hank's collections as the main focus.

One wall held a painting of golden desert poppies created by Georgia O'Keeffe. On a pedestal before it was a small bronze horse sculpted by Frederic Remington.

Reared on its hind legs, its front hooves beating the air in a moment of frozen power, each sinewy muscle straining, the horse evinced the wild freedom Hank admired about the Old West. The sculpture was Hank's favorite possession, and Tonia often saw him stand for a moment, running his hands over it. She had been impressed by Hank's pride of ownership where his art collection was concerned. He frequently loaned pieces to local museums for public view.

Besides the O'Keeffe poppies, paintings by Arizonan Ted DeGrazia, and one by the famous C. M. Russell, Hank had several done by a Navajo artist who he swore would become famous.

Tonia's favorite portrait was of a Navajo mother and child. She was drawn to it whenever she entered the room.

Rising, she walked to it now, admiring the Madonnalike quality of the mother's face.

The men's conversation stopped.

"Is that new, Hank?"

"No, Tonia's been here almost a month," his uncle answered guilelessly.

"You know what I mean."

"Yeah," Hank answered proudly. "That painting came into the Hedstrom gallery just after Tonia started working for me. Wesley Begay's work is getting better and better. I bought this one before his signature was even dry. I think I'll leave it to Tonia in my will. She loves it, and I can't see *you* with a Madonna on your living room wall."

Tonia's head sprang up to see Hank's eyes glittering with their usual devilish light.

Oh, don't do this to me, she thought in despair. Her gaze went to Ben's grim face. Hank's nephew already distrusted her enough, thanks to the older man's practical jokes. She shot Hank a warning look, which he ignored, and returned to her chair.

Ben continued to talk to his uncle, but his eyes were on her. "It's hard for me to believe *you've* got a Madonna and Child on your wall. You've always preferred Begay's wilder themes," he said, gesturing toward one painting in which several Navajo men on horseback were subduing a wild stallion.

"Well," Hank said, lifting one shoulder defensively. "Maybe I'm mellowing out."

The sip of coffee Tonia had just taken burned its way down. She jerked forward, gasping and coughing, and rattled her cup into its saucer. Both men leaped to their feet. Hank hurried over to pound her on the back.

She waved a weak hand at him. "I'm okay," she wheezed.

"Are you sure?" Hank asked, hovering over her, his hand still rubbing her back.

She nodded, embarrassed at the scene she was making. She had caught a glimpse of Ben's face as he watched the two of them. His eyes were fixed on Hank's soothing gestures.

After a few more pats to her back, Hank returned to his seat. Ben hesitated for a moment before resuming his.

Tonia looked over at her employer with glittering eyes. "Please don't use phrases like 'mellowing out' when I've got my mouth full."

Hank grinned at her reaction. "You like that? Heard it from a little kid I met on the beach the other day."

Tonia giggled, but Ben's steady gaze was moving from her to his uncle and back again.

Tonia thought his expression said "We are not amused."

When Hank didn't get a reaction out of his nephew, he looked a bit disappointed and asked Ben about the gala store opening in Chula Vista, which he planned to attend the next morning. In fact, he was to have the honor of cutting the ribbon at the new store's entrance.

Tonia half listened as she continued to study Hank's collections. The first time she had entered the room, she had been amazed that one person could collect so many things and keep them so well organized.

In glass-fronted cases that lined the walls, Hank had carefully labeled and indexed items of Western lore—the big eight-point star worn by the San Diego city police in the previous century, guns, knives of all types, and even a chunk of Billy the Kid's tombstone, taken during a midnight raid on the Fort Sumner, New Mexico, graveyard during Hank's teenage years.

Tonia wondered idly what Ben might collect. Rare books? No, something whose value was a little more showy. Pre-Columbian art, maybe.

Barely aware of the dreamy perusal she was giving the room—and especially Ben—Tonia looked up to meet his eyes.

Ben was listening to what Hank was saying, but his eyes were on Tonia.

"A party, Hank? Tomorrow night?"

"Yes. I've invited everyone in the neighborhood. We can use the occasion to celebrate your new store, too."

"But I didn't think you even knew most of the people around here."

"A good reason for inviting them to a get-together. Tonia has agreed to provide some of the evening's entertainment."

"Entertainment?"

Tonia's lips quirked, wondering if Ben was imagining her popping, barely clad, out of a cake.

"What kind of entertainment?"

"Fortune-telling," she told him, straightening in response to the suspicion in his voice. "Palmistry. You see, Ben, I am one of the Rom."

"The Rom?"

"I'm a Gypsy."

"EXACTLY WHAT have you told your nephew about me, Hank?"

Hank Tyson hunkered down behind the large, dusty volume he was reading, but he didn't answer. They were in the room behind their office that contained Hank's collection of books, newspapers and pamphlets. Built like a bank vault, the fireproof room had a controlled climate, no windows, and a heavy door that locked only from the outside.

"Ha-a-nk."

He looked up, all innocence. "Not much."

"On the beach yesterday Ben said you were planning to marry me."

"I didn't say that! I told him that I loved you. Said you were exactly the kind of girl I'd want to marry." Hank's eyes gleamed. "Course, you're too young for me."

"Then what was that 'this is the girl who's stolen my heart away' business?"

"Just trying to keep the young fool on his toes."

"What's that supposed to mean?"

"Nothing. Can't a man have any peace from his employees and relatives?"

"Not if what you do affects them, too."

His quick grin sparked light in his blue eyes. "You worry too much."

"What's *that* supposed to mean?"

"Never mind. Never mind. Got a date for my party?"

Tonia didn't like his expression so she decided to ask Paul Cortez to take her. They often did such favors for each other.

"Yes, I do."

Hank frowned. "Who? Someone special?"

"In a way." She smiled, remembering how Paul had helped her out whenever her car needed repairs and given her a shoulder to cry on when she had broken her engagement two years before. His sister, Maria, was her best friend, and he was the big brother she'd never had.

The corners of Hank's mouth deepened even more. "What's his name?"

"Paul Cortez."

His face cleared instantly. "Fine. Fine. Bring him along."

Now Tonia frowned. Hank was making noises like an overprotective father. "Now listen, Hank—"

"Don't you think we'd better get to work?" He pulled a large sheaf of notes from a file folder. "Now that we've got the format for the book determined, we can get started organizing the chapters." He stood and handed her the papers. "This is the information I've got on Cap Mossman and the Arizona Rangers for the section on state police. Just let me know if you can't read my writing."

She accepted the papers, but the direct look she gave him said the discussion wasn't over. The easy relationship they'd fallen into didn't mean he could pry into her personal life.

Tonia looked at the work Hank had given her. Within moments she was oblivious to her surroundings and to whatever trick his mind might be thinking up. She was deep in the previous century, reading observations made by the very astute founder of the Arizona Rangers. He had formed a band of twenty-six men, determined to keep peace in the territory.

She was eager to see how Hank would turn this work into narrative form. He seemed to have a natural understanding of the best way to formulate the book. His chapters followed one another in logical order, and the sections he had written so far were interesting, written with wit and flair. He sprinkled his own writing with quotations that brought his subjects to life in the reader's mind.

Hank's research methods fascinated her. She had already taken pages of notes to be used in the future when she was able to write on her own.

In spite of his love for practical jokes and the teasing way he treated her, Tonia respected his sharp mind. He seemed far younger than his sixty-five years, interested in learning new things and meeting new people.

She had encouraged his plan to have a party for his neighbors. He had told her he'd been depressed for a long time, but that his recent vacation had made him realize he was wasting his life, so he had decided to make some changes. He wanted to write his book before it was too late.

As she mulled it over, her unseeing eyes fixed on the cramped handwriting of a century ago, Tonia acknowledged how Hank's new lease on life could have worried his nephew. Ben had sent a depressed old man on a vacation and received a prankster in return. The symptoms could easily have been mistaken for those of an older man who had fallen in love with someone in her twenties.

Tonia looked up to see Hank watching her thoughtfully. Startled to be caught thinking about him, she made a face that caused him to burst out laughing.

"Why don't you come with me to the store opening tomorrow, Antonia?" he asked, leaning back in his chair.

"You mean the new one—Ben's store—in Chula Vista?"

"Yeah." Hank's eyes lit as he got caught up in the idea. "Lucy's thrilled I'm going to be out of the house so she and the caterers can get ready for my party. You might as well come, too."

"Well, I don't know...."

"What else do you have to do tomorrow, wash your hair? You're going to stand me up for that?"

Seeing the pained look on his face, Tonia hurried to re-assure him. "Of course not...."

"It's just for the morning. You'll have plenty of time to get ready for my party. Besides—" Hank's voice glowed with pride "—I know you'd like to see what my Ben has done with that store. You know, he's a good businessman. He picked a great manager who kept in touch by phone while Ben was in Arizona."

Tonia chewed her lip. She would like to see the family business. Although Hank was retired, he still kept an eye on what went on. And, why not admit it, she would like to see Ben in another setting.

"What time?"

"Bright and early," Hank said quickly, apparently fearing she would back out. "I'll pick you up at nine-thirty. The ceremonies start at ten."

With a gnawing feeling of apprehension, Tonia watched him rub his hands together. She hoped she hadn't just been suckered by his hurt expression.

CLUSTERS of red and white balloons emblazoned with the Tyson Auto Parts logo bobbed and danced in the spring breeze that swept around the new building. The smell of tar rushed up to greet her as Tonia stepped out of Hank's sporty new compact car. The freshly paved parking lot had a loose dusting of fine sand, giving it the appearance of having been touched with a powder puff.

Eagerly, she looked around at the activity. Free sodas and billed caps were being given away near the store's entrance.

Crowds of people, attracted by the fairlike atmosphere, milled around, waiting for the ceremonies to begin.

Tyson employees in candy-striped shirts and dark slacks rushed over to greet Hank, who shook each person's hand and called them by name.

"Where's Ben?" he asked a young woman with Assistant Manager embroidered on the pocket of her shirt.

"Over there," she answered, waving her hand vaguely in the direction of the store's entrance. "He's trying to get the rented PA system to work. Maybe you could help him—he's getting pretty hot under the collar."

Hank chuckled and followed the girl's directions, pulling Tonia with him.

On a small plywood platform, Ben was crouched behind a speaker box with a loose wire in his hand. As she and Hank approached, he picked up a screwdriver and began trying to attach the wire with slow, careful movements.

Tonia was surprised to see that he was wearing the same uniform as the other employees. If she had thought about it beforehand, she would have expected him to have on a suit as he had the day before.

"Need some help?" Hank asked, trying to peer over Ben's shoulder.

Without looking up, Ben grunted a greeting. "Do you think you could fix this, Hank? You know I've got more thumbs than fingers."

"The boy always was helpless," Hank said in an aside to Tonia. "Nearly cut off his hand in high school wood shop."

Ben whipped his head around to see who Hank was talking to. The gray eyes that had been concentrating on the speaker wire skidded up to level on Tonia's face. He stared at her for an instant before he slowly stood, his gaze raking over her appearance.

She had dressed in a magenta peasant dress, belted with a bright blue sash that matched her high heels and clutch bag. When Ben didn't speak, Tonia lifted her purse and tucked it under her arm, then stepped closer to Hank in a defensive gesture.

Irritated that Ben could make her feel on guard, she masked her feelings with a bright smile. "Good morning, Ben. This grand opening looks wonderful."

"There seems to be a good crowd. I'm glad you could make it," he said, sounding anything but glad. "Hey, Hank, do you think you could help me with this?" He moved between them, urging his uncle toward the speaker. Within moments he had Hank wrestling with the problem as he hovered nearby.

Left to herself, Tonia wandered over to the refreshment booth where she was given a complimentary cup of Coke. Sipping it, she moved around the edges of the crowd, stopping to enjoy a clown who was making balloon animals for a group of children. Nearby, a table of free samples was set up. A Tyson employee was giving away small bottles of polish and demonstrating its uses on a car parked behind him. Since she no longer had a car that ran, Tonia moved on.

Several times, she glanced over to see Hank and Ben working. Ben looked up once or twice to meet her eyes. She gave him her falsely bright smile and disappeared into the crowd.

Some Gypsies claimed to be able to read minds, but Tonia wasn't one of them. She wished she had that gift, though, to know what Ben was thinking. He didn't seem convinced that she wasn't trying to snare his uncle into a marital trap, but she refused to do any more explaining.

The public address system split the air with a shriek that had people covering their ears and wheeling around to see what the commotion was.

"Excuse me, folks," Ben said into the microphone. "That wasn't intentional, but I guess it got everyone's attention."

A ripple of laughter went through the crowd, and the people began moving closer to the small platform where Ben stood.

He thanked everyone for coming and said he hoped Tyson Auto Parts would be able to serve their car-care needs for many years to come.

He introduced Hank, who bounced up to the microphone carrying a large pair of scissors decorated with streamers. Mugging for his audience, he made a production of leading the way over to the front door, which was decorated with a huge ribbon and bow.

Hank held the large pair of scissors with a flourish and snipped at the ribbon.

It wouldn't cut on the first try. Tonia felt herself tensing while Hank sawed away at it. Finally he turned to the crowd and rolled his blue eyes skyward. "If Tyson sold scissors, we sure wouldn't carry this brand!"

Amid chuckles from the crowd, he managed to snip the ribbon, and threw open the doors to lead everyone inside.

Tonia stepped back, smiling fondly at him. Hank was in his element, directing people around the store, shaking hands and answering questions.

"Having fun?"

Tonia's smile froze as she turned her head to see Ben standing beside her. "Why, yes, I am. And Hank seems to love it."

Ben's steady gaze didn't flicker from her. "He loves this sort of thing. Although he was too sick to come to the opening of the El Cajon store a few months ago."

"Sick?" she asked, alarmed. "What was wrong?"

"He'd had the flu. Couldn't seem to get over it. His depression didn't help. I guess I've got you to thank that he seems cheered up. He hasn't really been himself since Aunt Maggie died."

Tonia's chin came up. "He's been exactly like this since I've known him. I'm only reaping the benefit of his good health since he's decided he feels well enough to write a book and hire an assistant," she said, putting the emphasis on the last word.

Lord, the man was stubborn, she thought, fuming. He couldn't seem to get it through his thick skull that there was nothing between her and his uncle.

Ben's eyes narrowed and he seemed about to speak, but Tonia hurried on. "Of course, you're benefiting from his good health, too," she added in a sincere tone that was patently false. "You can concentrate on business and not worry about him. That must be such a relief to you."

With a nod, she turned and walked away, leaving him to stare after her.

She located Hank, who said he was ready to leave. On the way to the car, her shoe slid on the loose sand that dusted the parking lot.

Hank grabbed her around the waist. "Careful, honey. I don't want my Gypsy fortune-teller in traction before the party."

Tonia grinned, steadying herself against him. She glanced up to see Ben watching them. He still had the unyielding expression he had worn almost constantly since they had met.

"I MUST ADMIT, you look the part." Ben was standing near the small table Tonia had set up to read the palms of Hank's guests. By ten o'clock that night the steady stream of fortune seekers had dwindled, and she was taking a break, sipping a glass of wine and people watching.

"Thank you," she finally said, trying to read his expression. "I find most people are receptive to having their fortunes told, especially if they don't have to take it too seriously."

He didn't answer, but his eyes roved over her. "You look very... exotic."

Tonia wasn't sure if he meant it as a compliment. She had worn a full black skirt with red, yellow and electric-blue flowers. Like the dress she had worn to the store opening that morning, her red blouse was peasant-style. This time she wore it low on her shoulders. Heavy gold necklaces and bracelets circled her throat and wrists, and big hoop earrings were fastened in her ears. She had enhanced her dark eyes with kohl and gray eye shadow so they looked sultry and mysterious. Around her head she had wound a red *diklo*, the traditional Gypsy headgear. The scarf fit her head like a cap and was tied at the back in a perky knot. From beneath the snug covering, her hair flowed around her shoulders in a curly black mass.

Her Aunt Yana would have had a fit. According to Romani tradition, unbound hair was the sign of a loose woman, and *diklos* were only worn by married ones, but no one here would know that.

"People expect a Gypsy to look exotic," Tonia answered Ben with a shrug. "Sit down—let me see what your hands tell me about you."

"So exotic, in fact, that I was surprised to see you at something as mundane as an auto-parts store," he went on.

Tonia folded her hands in front of her, giving herself a moment to think. "It *was* a grand opening," she reminded him. "I came because Hank invited me."

"Does he invite you many places?"

Anger sparked in Tonia's eyes. She decided to give him something to really make him suspicious. She leaned forward, peering about as if afraid of being overheard. "Well," she stage-whispered. "He's never taken me to a topless bar."

Stunned, he stared at her for a moment before allowing a smile to twitch at the corner of his mouth.

A bit nonplussed by her triumph over him, Tonia pointed to the chair again. "Sit down. Let me read your palm."

Ben hesitated, his gaze going across the room to where he had left his date. The beautiful blonde was chatting happily with Hank and a star-struck Paul Cortez.

"She looks well taken care of. Perhaps she would like her palm read later."

Ben grinned. "That probably won't be necessary. Chloe knows exactly what her future holds."

"I'll bet."

"Don't let appearances fool you, Miss Meier. Chloe will get whatever she wants because she's one of the best investment counselors in San Diego."

Tonia had the grace to blush. "How nice for her."

"Tell me, Antonia, have very many of Hank's guests crossed your palm with silver to have their fortunes told?"

She bridled. "I'm doing this for fun. Free. Gratis, because Hank asked me to."

"Why did you decide to become a Gypsy?" he asked. "Did you have childhood dreams of running away to join a band of wanderers?"

She sighed. "No. I had childhood dreams of running away to live in a real home instead of a trailer."

"What do you mean?" he asked, finally accepting the chair she had offered.

"Ben, Gypsies are born, not made," she explained as she had done so many times before. "We are an ethnic group just like any other. We have tribes and families within each tribe. We speak the Romani language, have our own customs and culture."

"But traditionally, don't Gypsies—"

"Poach, pilfer and prevaricate? Sometimes."

"And you're proud of that?"

"Proud of being one of the Rom, yes. But not proud of all our ways. There are many things I'd like to change."

"What things?"

"The lack of a history of the Gypsies and their customs written by one of the Rom," she answered proudly. "The techniques we develop researching and writing Hank's book about Western lawmen will help me with my book on the Rom."

"Oh," he said slowly, his eyes reflective. "I see. So when Ben decided to write this book, you were ready..."

Tonia stared at him, waiting for him to continue. When he didn't, she prompted him. "What do you mean, Ben?"

Her question brought his gaze back to hers. He smiled in a way she thought she could come to hate because it hid his thoughts. "Never mind. Weren't you going to read my palm?" He rested the backs of his hands on the table.

Tonia stared at him for a moment before she took hold of them and turned them over. Dark blond hairs dusted their backs, deepening to ash-brown at his wrists.

"What, no crystal ball?"

She barely heard him. "Another myth, Ben. Gypsies have never used them."

Tonia turned his hands over, studied both palms and finally held the right one up for closer examination. "A good palmist really needs a couple of hours' study to know a person through their palm."

He seemed amused. "Do you think you'll know me in a few minutes?"

She answered solemnly. "I couldn't know you in a lifetime."

He blinked in surprise and she shifted her eyes back to his hand. She ran her fingers over the base of his thumb. His skin was warm and firm. No calluses marred it, but his weren't the hands of a lazy man. Energy flowed from them. "Your Mount of Venus line is firm and well rounded indicating good health, a lot of energy—and a strong sex drive." Involuntarily, her gaze slid to Chloe and then back to Ben.

He grinned at her.

She cleared her throat. "Ah—well, the number of lines raying out here indicate strong creative energies."

The grin widened.

Her eyes were on his hand as she touched the base of his first finger. "The Mount of Jupiter and your index finger indicate you are ambitious and a good leader. This is enhanced by your Mount of Mars, here on the outside, which also signals your aggressiveness. Your fingers are rather short for a man of your height, telling me you tend to be impatient. You don't suffer fools gladly."

Tonia hesitated before uttering her next words. Her gaze met his watchful eyes, lingered on his high forehead, straight nose and sensually molded lips. "You are very sensuous. You like the feel of things. Softness, comfort—appeal to you."

Ben drew in a quick breath at the rapt expression on her face. Her deep brown eyes pulled him forward. No woman had ever looked at him as if she wanted to know him inside and out, and even though he knew she did it with all her subjects, it appealed to him.

Her eyes finally left his face. "Your Mount of Apollo and adjoining finger indicate financial success," she continued, touching his third finger. "You will be very wealthy."

It was a statement with little interest behind it.

"Mercury indicates you are exceptionally intelligent and shrewd but highly egotistical."

"Hey!"

"You hate looking foolish, so as a child you probably tended to strike first, before someone could hurt you. You still do this with words." Her finger ran the length of the line that bisected his palm. "This is backed up by your head line. The way that line tangles here—" she touched the center of his palm "—with your life line shows that you are very cautious about making decisions, and sadly, that it is very difficult for you to trust people."

Her eyes lifted to his once again. They held a faraway look. "And that is strange because even though you're cautious about decisions, you also make snap judgments. Too bad," she sighed. "But I suppose it's because you were very badly hurt once, years ago."

"Did Hank tell you that?" Ben growled.

"No, Hank has told me almost nothing about you."

"Sure. Listen, Tonia, I think I've heard—"

"I'm almost finished." She gripped his wrist and went back to studying his palm. "The fact that your heart line runs in a steady, unbroken sweep from below Mercury between the fingers of Jupiter and Saturn shows you have a healthy, physical attitude about—sex. You are somewhat fickle now, but when you fall in love, it will be for life."

"Fickle!"

"Ben, I'm only reading what's right here for anyone to see," she said reasonably, but couldn't keep down the hint of laughter in her eyes. "Have I said anything at all that isn't true?"

"I've heard enough of this." Ben pushed back his chair. "Let's dance."

Tonia grinned. "What a gracious invitation, but what if more people want a reading?"

"They can wait. I'm sure Hank didn't invite you just to provide the entertainment."

"All right, then. I'd like to dance."

While they had been talking, the tape of rock music had been replaced by one of slow tunes. Ben led her to the dance floor that had been created by moving out some of Hank's furniture and pushing the remainder against the wall. Tonia went into Ben's arms, resting one hand at his shoulder and allowing her other to be swallowed by his larger one.

She couldn't quite decide why she liked being in his arms. His mood toward her swept from suspicion to hostility and back again, but being near him was exciting.

Their hands, bodies, steps fit well together.

Tonia liked the feel of his heavy knit sweater and the hardness of his neck muscles beneath her touch. Her fingers flexed, wanting to touch more of him. She could have rested her head easily on his chest, but instead she tilted it back and looked up at him.

"Hank's party seems to be a success. I take it he doesn't do this often?"

Ben frowned. "Not since Aunt Maggie died. And never one like this."

"People change, Ben."

"This isn't a change, Tonia. It's a major revolution!" He didn't seem to want to say any more, so Tonia just enjoyed the dance. When it was over, he slid his hand down her arm to catch her fingers in his. "Let's get out of here."

He began leading her toward the redwood deck overlooking the ocean.

"Won't your date miss you, Ben?"

"Well, what else could I do?" Tonia asked, spreading her hands theatrically. "Leave him there for all the world to gloat over? He wasn't very popular in the neighborhood—he was so noisy—but he deserved a better fate than to be left right out in public!"

Ben thrust a trembling hand through his hair. "Well, y-yes, I guess so, but what did the people from the mortuary say?"

Tonia looked up, her lips twitching. She hoped it looked as if it was from grief. "Nothing. You see, I didn't call them."

"Didn't call them! What did you do with him?"

Her lashes batted over the innocent expression in her ebony eyes. "Why, he's still there."

"In the *garage*!"

Ben's eyes were almost popping from his head, his face was flushed red, and he was breathing hard. So that's what it means to look apoplectic, she thought.

"Of course," she said calmly, pushing away from the railing. "Where else would one keep a fourteen-year-old Volkswagen that won't run anymore?"

Ben's expression was frozen halfway between tragedy and comedy. "A what?" he wheezed.

"A broken-down car, Ben. You overheard a conversation about a car and jumped to conclusions." Tonia clucked her tongue and shook her head. "It's because of those tangled head and life lines. You just can't trust."

She straightened and jabbed him to emphasize every word she said. Her cool, amused control began to crumble away before the hurt she felt. He barely knew her but was prepared to think the worst of her. Embarrassed that she had been even momentarily attracted to him, she lashed out.

"I don't really care—" her finger dug into his chest "—what you think of me, Mr. Andrews. I don't—" she poked him again "—work for you, and I don't have to answer to you. But just in case you have any more worries about me casting spells on Hank—" With shaking fingers, she pulled a strand of red yarn from the fringe of her shawl. "Here."

"What's this?" His voice was raspy.

"To keep someone free of a Gypsy curse, put a red string around his finger. It works even better than garlic or wolfsbane! Now you tie this around Hank's finger, and he'll be perfectly safe from me. Of course, he'll probably laugh in your face."

With that she spun around and reentered the living room.

Inside, Tonia took a few minutes to compose herself before returning to her table. Several people were waiting to have their palms read, and she dispatched them quickly with a few well-practiced phrases that promised long life and happiness.

Ben came in from the deck and started once again for her table, but she froze him with a look. He went to the bar, which was set up in a corner, and poured himself a drink.

"Tonia?"

She had been so intent on watching Ben that she hadn't seen Lucy Heller standing beside her table with two men. "Hello, Lucy," she greeted Hank's young housekeeper. "You've done a wonderful job here tonight."

The girl flushed with pleasure. "It was mostly the caterers."

She drew one of the men a little closer, and Tonia looked at him fully. He had dark hair, and a thin mustache. His eyes constantly roamed the room as if mentally adding up the worth of everyone there.

"Tonia, I want you to meet my brother, George. He's been away. Hank said it was all right if he came tonight."

"Yes, I can see the family resemblance," Tonia commented. Their features were similar, but Lucy had pale blond hair and eyes of topaz, while her brother was swarthy. "How do you do, George?"

He barely grunted an answer, his gaze lingering on her for an uncomfortably long instant before roaming the room again.

Suppressing a shiver, Tonia turned to Lucy's other companion.

"And this is Melvin Morris," Lucy said, pulling him forward. From the worshipful look on Lucy's face, Tonia decided he was the girl's boyfriend.

Melvin offered a limp hand for her to shake. He was blond, with eyebrows and lashes so pale that his face looked naked. His eyes were of the lightest blue.

"Tonia, do you think Hank will mind that I invited Dr. Justin, too? He's interested in meeting Hank in person and seeing his collections."

"Hank won't care. He loves showing his treasures." Tonia tilted her head to one side and regarded Lucy. "How did you meet Dr. Justin? I thought your major was nutrition. Did you take one of his anthropology classes as an elective?"

"No. George and Melvin work in the shop Dr. Justin just opened in Old Town." Lucy smiled at the two young men listening. George just stared at his sister, but Melvin offered a weak smile in return.

Tonia had heard of the gift shop the professor had opened in the oldest section of San Diego. It featured a collection of Central and South American arts and crafts. Some were strictly tourist fare while other pieces were very valuable. "It sounds like we all need to thank Dr. Justin. He's a one-man employment agency."

Lucy laughed her agreement, but neither man responded to Tonia's feeble joke.

"Tonia." Hank hailed her from several feet away. "Come dance with me." Tonia turned toward him, grateful to escape Lucy's unnerving companions. Making conversation with them was impossible.

Hank's face glowed with pleasure and a fine film of perspiration. "Lucy taught me some new steps, and I've been practicing." He threw his young housekeeper a teasing look and laughed when she blushed. George and Melvin watched Hank warily.

"Don't you think you might be overdoing it, Hank?" Tonia asked, frowning her concern.

"Nonsense. I feel fine. You know, a person isn't old until he starts to think old. Come on." He grabbed her hand and whirled her away.

Hank led her in a galloping dance. After a few minutes the others fell back, until the middle-aged man and the whirling Gypsy had an enthusiastic audience around the edges of the room.

Tonia's black hair flew out like an unfurled cape as she twirled faster and faster. Laughing, Hank stepped back and let her dance alone. Caught up in the beat and excitement of the piece she broke into a complicated series of steps that was redolent of Gypsy camps hidden in deep forest glades. Her feet, in high heels, pounded out a flamencolike rhythm. Hands lifted, her fingers snapped to the beat. She wished she had her castanets. As it was, she felt the exhilarating freedom she always experienced when she danced. All that mattered was the twisting, turning movements—the sound, the feel, the dance.

WITH GRUDGING FASCINATION, Ben watched Tonia's performance. Her small, quick body twirled so fast she was a blur of black and red, with an occasional glimpse of her slim legs when she kicked her skirt high.

telling her all this. He couldn't be thinking that *she* would make a good mother for the grandchildren he wanted! Hank was eccentric, not crazy. "Hank—"

"Tonia, do you know anything about that guy with Lucy?"

Tonia followed his gaze to where Lucy was dancing with the blond young man.

"Her brother?"

"No, the one she's dancing with."

"Melvin Morris. Her boyfriend, I think." She turned back to the buffet.

"Yeah, he brought her to work one day."

"He seems very—" Tonia's tongue tripped over the word "insipid" and finally came out with "—polite."

"Hmph. I'll wager he's got a second-rate personality with a third-rate one trying hard to surface."

"Hank!"

He turned shrewd blue eyes on her. "Have you read his palm yet?"

"No."

"See if you can. It might help us."

"Do what? And what do you mean 'us'?"

"Why, help us get to know him, of course," Hank answered her first question innocently and ignored the second one.

Tonia gaped at him. "Hank, you aren't trying to play matchmaker, are you?" Tonia's mind reeled. He couldn't think Lucy would make a good wife for Ben. He would chew the poor girl up and spit her out!

"Nah," he snorted. "She's a nice kid. I just want to know if this Melvin is good enough for her. She's waving at us. It looks like there's somebody she wants us to meet."

Tonia turned around again. "Dr. Justin!" She grabbed Hank's arm, pulling him through the crowd to introduce the two men.

As they talked, Tonia watched Dr. Justin with indulgent amusement. She seldom saw him since she'd finished his classes, but he hadn't changed. His clothes were flamboyant, giving him the air of an aging Regency rake. He wore a loose cashmere jacket and slacks, white satin shirt and a long silk scarf knotted at his throat over several gold chains. A jaunty beret was perched on his balding head.

Otis Justin had very expensive tastes and liked to indulge them. This wasn't easy on a college professor's salary, and it had been rumored on campus that he'd made a killing in an investment scheme that was barely this side of legal. He was an excellent teacher, though, as well as friendly and likable and if Tonia was occasionally bothered by the shrewd gleam she saw in his eyes, she accepted it as part of his complex personality.

"It's good to see you, Dr. Justin. I want to thank you again for recommending me for this job."

"Oh, I didn't really—"

"Dr. Justin—Otis," Hank interrupted. "Why don't you come over here and I'll tell you all about my collections. And we'll get you a drink." Hank all but frog-marched the professor away.

Tonia turned back to her fortune-telling table but forgot about Hank and Dr. Justin when she saw Ben and Chloe dancing together. Her hands were laced together at the back of his neck, her fingers stealing up through his hair. Ben's hands were similarly clasped at Chloe's waist, bringing their hips together.

Trying to understand her confusing feelings about Ben, she considered what Hank had told her. The story of Ben's college romance, coupled with what she'd seen in his palm, explained his suspicions. Now she felt a little ashamed of the scene on the terrace. True, he had eavesdropped on her telephone conversation, but he thought he was protecting Hank. It occurred to her that he might go to great lengths to protect his uncle. She admitted to herself that she already knew that. His palm had told her he didn't like to look foolish. That, no doubt, applied to those he cared about, too.

At the small table by the window, Paul Cortez slumped in a chair, looking pretty much the way she felt, but he stood when she approached and coaxed her to dance.

Paul whirled her past Hank and Dr. Justin at one point, and she smiled to see how they had hit it off.

"Insurance? Of course," Hank was saying. "But I've got a great security system...."

When Paul returned her to her table, Lucy was there with Melvin in tow. Tonia read his palm and discovered that the blandness of his personality went all the way through. He was a hero-worshiper, idolizing those he thought were smarter or stronger than himself. Tonia decided she didn't have much to report to Hank.

The party began winding down a couple of hours later, and Paul drove her home. He gave her a glowing account of Chloe's attributes, and she went to bed that night thinking of Ben making love to the elegant blonde. She groaned, buried her head under the pillow and willed herself to sleep.

THE RINGING PHONE roused Tonia the next morning, and she reached out a flailing arm to cradle the curved plastic against her collarbone. "H'lo?"

"Antonia, my *shey*! What is the matter with you?"

"Mamio?" Tonia yawned into the receiver and smiled, warmed by the sound of her mother's voice and the Ro-

mani term for beloved child. "Nothing's wrong. I was out late last night."

"A date!" Annie Meier exclaimed. "You had a date?"

"Sort of. Paul Cortez and I went to a party."

"Oh, him." Her mother didn't bother to disguise her disappointment. "I thought you meant with a possible husband. Wouldn't you like to be engaged to some nice young man? I wouldn't even expect much of a *daro*," Annie Meier added magnanimously.

Tonia rolled onto her back and smiled at the ceiling remembering Hank's concern that Ben get married. Parents were pretty much alike no matter what their backgrounds, she decided.

"Mother, for a forward-thinking woman you have some very old-fashioned ideas. It's no longer necessary to pay a bride price. And what if I married a *gajo*? A non-Gypsy wouldn't want to pay a *daro*."

"I wouldn't mind at all if you married a non-Gypsy. I was raised by one, remember?"

"I know, Mother. But there is no possibility of a *Zamutro* for you in the near future. Understand—no son-in-law! Besides, I didn't know you were so anxious to get a son-in-law."

Mrs. Meier sighed, "Well, I guess I'll just have to come home and help you look. If I'd been more aware of what was going on two years ago you might never have become engaged to that disgusting Greg."

Tonia ignored the reference to her past mistake. "Don't you dare come home early, *Mamio*! You deserve a vacation. How is Mrs. Marks?"

Asking about her mother's old friend was a guaranteed way of getting her off the subject of a husband for Tonia. They talked for several minutes about Tonia's job and especially her boss. Annie wanted to hear all about the party and laughed at the description of Hank learning to disco. Tonia hung up, glad she had been able to distract her mother's matchmaking schemes.

Tonia reveled in the new vigor in her mother's voice. She had noticed the marked improvement about a month ago. Their phone conversations had begun to center less on Grandpa Joe and more on the sights Annie was seeing, the people she had met and news about Tonia's job.

Although she took it as a good sign that her mother was once again interested in life, Tonia didn't think she was ready for interference in her own love life—or lack of one.

Sitting on the side of the bed, Tonia looked out at the old pepper tree in the backyard. Year-round, it constantly lost and renewed its leaves. It sent out runners, establishing new shoots all over the lawn, eager to procreate. She wondered if parents, when they attained a certain age, wanted the same for their children. If so, both Hank and her mother had reached it!

MONDAY MORNING Tonia was in the vault room. For an hour she had been deep in a search for references to Joe Phy, Arizona lawman.

A shadow fell across the small worktable she had set up as close as possible to the open door. She gasped and jerked back. "Ben, you scared me!"

He grimaced and smoothed his palms over the vest he wore with his dark blue tailored suit. "I'm sorry. I just dropped by to see if you might be willing to listen to an apology."

She turned in her chair and leaned back. "I'm always willing to listen to something like that. Do you know anybody interested in making one?"

A reluctant grin tipped up one corner of his mouth. He took off his glasses and slipped them into his jacket pocket. "You've always got a smart answer, don't you?"

"Not always."

"That was quite a performance you put on the other night. I laughed about it later."

Laughed about it? With Chloe? Her gaze wavered. "I was embarrassed about the way I put you on. Acting comes naturally to me." Her shoulders lifted in a self-deprecating shrug. "Remember, we Gypsies have been perfecting the art of deceiving *gajes*—that's you—for hundreds of years." She met his eyes. "I was furious about what you thought of me."

"I've thought a lot about what has happened in the past few days—and about what you said Saturday night. I guess I let my imagination run away with me. I've felt responsible for Hank for a long time." He paused and ran his hand around the back of his neck. "But, believe me, this new Hank is going to take some getting used to. Understand?"

"Of course. I appreciate your concern for Hank. I feel silly giving you advice about your own uncle, but don't take him too seriously."

"I'll try to remember that," Ben said, smiling. His gray eyes looked warmer than she'd ever seen them, and hers were drawn to them.

She was reluctant to trust this change in him, but he seemed as uncertain about it as she did. Smiling, she turned back to her work.

"What are you doing?" One of his compact hands waved toward the papers on the worktable.

She explained about her search for information on Joe Phy. "I just found a newspaper article about Wyatt Earp that Hank had misplaced. Did you know Earp ran gambling casinos in San Diego in the 1880s? He also refereed prize fights. Look.''

Ben followed her over to the file cabinet and watched as she drew a yellowed copy of the *San Diego Union* from a drawer and pointed out the article.

"Congratulations. I'm sure Hank was glad you found it."

"He doesn't know yet. He took Lucy to the market on his way to the office supply store...." Tonia's voice faltered as she looked up into Ben's face.

Teasing humor leaped into his eyes. It reminded her of the way they had gleamed at her when she had read his palm, laughing at her embarrassed assessment of his sex drive. The uncertainty he'd seemed to experience moments before had disappeared. And that made her very nervous!

"Miss Meier, does that mean—do I dare hope—that we are alone?"

"Why do you want to know?"

"Ah, so cautious. You weren't afraid of me Saturday night on the terrace...."

"There were a hundred people in the living room."

"And you handled yourself very well."

"It's you I'm worried about handling!" she exclaimed on a breathless laugh.

"Worried, huh? Well, I'll just have to see about that." Ben's voice had dropped to a disturbing purr that sent her heart slamming against her ribs. He moved a few inches closer. She retreated from the wickedly grinning face drawing nearer in the darkening room. Darkening!

Frantic, she spun around.

The vault door was shutting!

"Oh no!" Tonia darted past Ben and virtually leaped across the room. She threw herself against the heavy metal door.

"Tonia!"

Her hands scrabbled frantically at the knob while she shoved with her shoulder and hip. "Help me, Ben. I can't get it open!"

Reacting to her panic, he was beside her in an instant. "Just calm down, Tonia. It'll be all right," he soothed, pushing against the door. Muscles bulged in his arms and neck as he heaved upward on the handle.

"Why am I doing this?" he asked in self-mockery. "It won't open from the inside. It's a security lock. Hank'll be home soon, won't he? When he sees the door is shut, he'll open it."

Tonia began shaking, her breath shallow. "I know, but isn't there something we can do? I can't stand to be closed up in here!" Fright clawed its way up her throat. "Oh, how did this happen? I just know I had it propped open...."

"If this is another one of Hank's practical jokes, I'll kill him."

"No, no," she gasped. "He wouldn't shut the vault."

Ben's hands came out to gently cup her shoulders. "Tonia, take it easy. Do you have claustrophobia?"

She nodded her head and squeezed her eyes shut. "Since I...was a child. A play...mate locked me...in a closet by accident...then ran away scared. Do you have any idea...how small the closet in a house trailer is?" Her voice became a wail. "Most of the time I can handle it. I can prepare myself when I have to go in an elevator, you know? But this...."

With a sympathetic noise deep in his throat, Ben pulled her against him. One hand speared through the curly black mass of her hair to massage her scalp in soothing circles. He murmured quiet phrases as he bent and caught her, one arm across her back, the other beneath her knees, swinging her up into his arms.

"Let's sit down and talk about this. It's not as bad as you think. Look, we'll turn on all the lights." He flipped them on as he spoke, trying to nudge her head back with his chin, but she had buried her face against his throat, her eyes shut tight. "The room is small but not tiny."

Tonia made a choked sound of distress and Ben cursed. "Bad choice of words, huh?"

"Y-yes."

"We'll sit down. I'll hold you. Don't worry, I won't let anything happen to you." He carried her to a small armchair Hank often used and sat down with her on his lap. He wrapped his arms loosely around her. "Look on the bright side. We have light, each other to talk to—you have something to drink." He nodded toward a cup of coffee she'd left on the worktable.

"What if I need to go to the bathroom?" She sounded serious and forlorn.

Ben cleared his throat and swallowed rapidly several times. "I'm sorry, darling. There's nothing I can do about that!"

Recognizing the choked tone of his voice, Tonia tilted her head back and glared at him. "It's not funny."

Instantly contrite, Ben lifted a hand and smoothed the back of it over her pale cheek, then pushed strands of midnight hair away from her face. "No. It isn't funny. I'm sorry." He fell silent, his hand against her face, his eyes staring into hers.

As she watched, his pupils widened as though in pleasure. "Tonia, I think I'm going to have to do something to take your mind off our situation."

"Oh?"

Ben had seen her laughing, angry, excited, and now frightened and vulnerable. In that moment she was both incredibly childlike and undeniably sexy. He thought about the way she had danced at Hank's party and the promise he had felt from her. Although he knew his timing stank, he decided to claim the promise.

Tonia was beautiful. The whiteness of her face was stark against her black hair. The red of her lips was an inviting bow in her face. He lowered his head until his lips were resting lightly on hers.

"Ben," she gasped, shock replacing her earlier fright. "What—what are you doing?"

"Honey, if you have to be told, I must not be doing it right. I'll just keep at it, and you let me know when you figure it out." His gently mocking laughter puffed against her lips just before he fused her mouth with his own.

For an instant Tonia was too stunned to respond, but his tentative touch, his warmth and comfort were persuasive, and she slipped her arms around his neck. His mouth moved on hers, nipping, exploring, tasting....

Ben pulled his lips from hers and drew in a great shuddering breath.

"I've figured it out," she gasped.

"Oh?"

"Mm-hmm, but I think I need a little more experience just to be sure."

"Ah, Tonia."

He kissed her again, and the memory of any other man who had ever held her was burned away in the heat of Ben's sensuality. As his kiss deepened, his fingers slid over her cheeks and into the soft curls of her hair. They found the sensitive spot at the nape of her neck and massaged it, sending ripples of pleasure through her.

"I'm going to name my next car Ben," Tonia murmured, drawing away from him for a moment.

"What?"

"When I was sixteen I named my car after the best kisser I'd ever dated," she said dreamily, her throbbing lips curved into a seductive smile. "But you're much better than Ralph was."

Ben laughed and hugged her tightly to him. "Lord, woman, what a thing to say to a man!" He drew her closer and began kissing her once again.

"Tonia, you taste wonderful," he groaned against the skin of her throat. "Like no one else."

Tonia thought that the heat building up in her couldn't keep spiraling out of control like this without some catastrophic effect. She was both scared and unbearably aroused.

She cupped her hands around his jaw and drew his face away from her throat. "Ben—we've got to stop this."

He cocked an eyebrow at her, his eyes silvery with desire and delight. "Give me one good reason why we should?"

Ben looked so appealing, Tonia answered on a breathy laugh, "Come to think of it, I can't come up with even one...." She lowered her mouth back to his.

They were so wrapped up in each other and the delight they were finding, that for a moment neither of them heard the sounds on the other side of the vault door. Finally the click of lock tumblers penetrated the sensuous haze they had created around themselves.

"Tonia, listen," Ben said, pulling his mouth from hers reluctantly.

"Mmm, what is it?"

"Someone's opening the door. It must be Hank."

"Oh—no!" She realized how disheveled she was. She leaped off Ben's lap and began stuffing her blouse into the waistband of her bright skirt. "Ben, do I look... debauched?"

He grinned. "You look like you've been thoroughly kissed by a man who knows what he's doing."

"Oh, you're conceited!" She tottered over to the door, his low chuckle following her.

She reached the door just as it swung open, and she tumbled out into Hank's waiting arms.

"Tonia, honey, are you all right? Look, Lucy, her face is all red. Quick, get a glass of water."

Lucy ran from the room, and a frightened Hank hustled Tonia to the sofa in the corner of the office. He had her lying back on the leather couch and was rubbing her hands vigorously before she knew what was happening. "Honey, I'm so sorry. I don't know how that door got shut. Lucy and I both gone—you locked up in there. I know how you hate being in little places...."

"She's all right, Uncle Hank."

The deep voice speaking from the vault doorway jerked Hank around. "Ben, what are you doing here?"

He shrugged and sauntered into the room. "I just dropped by. We were in the vault talking when the door shut. Tonia was upset at first, but then she was able to stop thinking about it."

Tonia groaned and turned the deepest possible shade of red. Next he would probably tell Hank how he'd helped distract her from her claustrophobia. She closed her eyes, trying to think of words to tell him what she thought of him.

At that moment a frantic Lucy rushed into the room carrying a full glass of water. She dashed over to the sofa and threw the contents of the glass into Tonia's face.

"Aargh!" Tonia shrieked and jumped up, slapping at the water.

"Lucy, girl. I meant for Tonia to drink the water, not wear it."

Lucy tightened her hands around the glass and burst into tears. "I'm sorry! She had her eyes closed, and I thought she had fainted."

Ben walked over to Tonia, pulling a handkerchief from his pocket, caught her jaw in his palm and began wiping her face. "No harm done, Lucy. Why don't you go get her a towel?"

"Oh, of course." She rushed from the room.

Hank came over and offered his handkerchief. His lined face was twitching uncontrollably.

The water had soaked Tonia's blouse and run down her throat to pool in the indentation between her breasts, trapped there by her bra. She dabbed at her neck with the drenched handkerchiefs and longed to wipe up the little puddle. Oh, what the heck, she thought, and turning her back, pulled her bra away from her skin to let the water run down her stomach. She blotted at it with the dry tail of her blouse.

She turned back to see Ben and Hank carefully avoiding looking at each other. Both men were almost purple in the face from trying to hold back laughter, cheeks puffed out and eyes nearly popping from their heads with the effort.

"Don't you laugh," she warned. "Don't you dare laugh!"

But their eyes slid to each other, met, and both men burst into hearty guffaws, their arms looped around each other's necks.

Tonia was so furious that she should have dried off instantly from the heat of her anger. "Oh, you think that's funny, huh?"

Two pairs of eyes swung to her, then to each other. Ben and Hank nodded and started laughing all the harder. Her anger burned white-hot for another instant but then began to cool. Well, she might have laughed, too, if it hadn't happened to her.

Lucy hurried back with the towels, and Tonia stalked away to dry off and find something to wear in place of her saturated blouse.

A few minutes later she returned to the den wearing a shirt she'd found in the downstairs hall closet. The dark blue garment was huge on her and clashed wildly with her purple-and-yellow striped skirt, but at least she was decently covered until her blouse and bra dried. She found Hank and Ben checking the hinges on the vault door.

"I don't know how it shut by itself," Ben was saying. "Tonia and I were standing by the file cabinet so we didn't really see anything."

Hank shook his head. "Well, I'm going to have the firm that installed it come out and take a look. I don't want this to happen again."

Both men straightened and turned to see Tonia at the door. Ben chuckled. "Hello, water baby. You look a lot better in that shirt than I ever did."

She sniffed. "If I'd known it was yours, I wouldn't have worn it. Now, if you two are finished laughing at me, I'll get back to work."

"Yes, ma'am. This has been a stimulating morning, but I've got to get back to the mundane business world," Ben said.

Tonia grimaced at his emphasis on the word "stimulating." She knew what he was thinking and excused her own behavior in the vault by remembering her fear and emotional stress.

Hank had walked over to his desk and picked up the bag from the office-supply store. He frowned down at the top of his desk. "Tonia, where's that bibliography?"

She pulled her eyes away from Ben's wickedly gleaming ones. "I don't know, Hank. I haven't been using it."

"It was right here," he said, beginning to search through a small pile of papers on the desk. "A bound manila folder. About so thick—" he held his thumb and forefinger half an inch apart.

"I know what it looks like. The last time I saw it, you'd put it on the desk." Tonia went over to help him search.

"Yes, right here, just before Lucy and I went to the store. We've got to find it. It's the list of my whole collection. Hundreds of books...."

"I know, Hank," she soothed. "We'll find it."

"I'll help," Ben volunteered, and the three of them looked in the office and the vault.

"Nothing," Tonia announced a few minutes later.

"It wasn't your only copy, was it, Uncle Hank?"

"No, no. But I don't like not knowing what became of it. Funny, it's like the darn thing just walked off."

"Maybe it did," Ben said quietly, and Tonia looked up to see that his speculative gaze was on her.

CHAPTER FOUR

"ARE YOU GOING TO BROOD all day, or do you think we could get some work done?"

Hank's voice, coming from the office doorway, caused Tonia to jump and drop the pen she had been toying with.

Her blouse had dried so she was once again dressed in her own clothes. She had pulled her hair back into a demure French braid and freshened her makeup. Nothing about her neat appearance showed how shaky she was on the inside.

"Sorry, Antonia, didn't mean to scare you," Hank said gruffly, then snorted. "I sound like an old grizzly bear with a sore paw."

"We'll find the bibliography." She rose from her chair and walked over to lay a hand on his arm. Her dark eyes were warm with sympathy.

"Yeah, yeah, I know." A gnarled hand came up to pat hers awkwardly. "But I hate losing things. It makes me feel like a senile old coot."

He looked so downcast Tonia burst out laughing. "I can't imagine anyone who shows his age less," she declared. "And I live in a neighborhood with lots of older people."

Hank favored her with a perky grin. "Oh, yeah?"

"Yeah," she said, giving his arm a squeeze.

"And you don't think I'm getting senile?"

"Heavens, no!"

"Good," he smiled. "I've got a reason to stay young...."

"You mean the book?"

He gave a shrug and flashed her a coy look. "That, among other things."

She laughed at the way he enjoyed secrets and mysteries. "Hank, you'll never grow old."

That seemed to cheer him, and they got down to work transcribing some of his notes into readable form.

Several times during the day Tonia thought about Ben, wondering what had been in his mind when he left. If he suspected her of taking Hank's list, she was very disappointed in him. If he thought she had made the vault door close so someone else could take the bibliography, he was crazy. No one with claustrophobia shut themselves up voluntarily.

Unless he thought she had faked that, too.

She forced her mind to stop going in circles, trying to second-guess him. He would think whatever he pleased, eventually drawing his own conclusions.

Her face burned at the memory of how she had responded to his kisses. She would just have to keep her distance, she decided. She had felt off kilter since meeting him.

With that decided, she settled down to work and typed several pages of notes.

Late in the afternoon Hank pulled a box of his rare books from a closet and placed it on the desk. "There's a book-restoring-and-binding firm in Kearny Mesa. Can you take these there on your way home?"

"Sure," she answered, reaching for the phone. "I'll call a cab."

"Where's your car?"

"Sick."

"Hmph, didn't know that." Hank fished out his keys and started removing one from the ring. "You'll use one of mine until yours is fixed."

"Oh, Hank, I couldn't."

"Sure you can. I can't drive two at the same time and we—I mean I—won't be needing this one for a few weeks."

Although she was reluctant to accept, knowing what Ben would think, Tonia allowed herself to be convinced. What Hank did with his cars was none of Ben's business. At four-thirty that afternoon she found herself driving home in the car Hank had driven to the grand opening of Ben's new store.

SHE DIDN'T SEE BEN for the rest of the week, and she was able to enter the vault with most of her fears at bay. She was grateful to him for that at least, and her feeling of disappointment in him had faded.

Her resolution to keep her distance from him was tested when he strolled in late one afternoon. Wearing dark slacks and a sport coat with a gray sweater that matched his eyes, he looked as though he had just stepped off one of the sailboats she could see fighting the wind out on the water. As he walked into the room, he lifted one hand and settled his hair into place, then took off his glasses and slipped them into his jacket pocket.

She smiled at the characteristic gesture, wondering if he even realized how often he took them on and off.

She was kneeling behind one of the display cases. Hank had asked her to rearrange some of his Western artifacts. He wanted to make room for a set of hunting knives he had gleefully unearthed at an estate sale.

Sitting back on her heels, Tonia was able to observe Ben and remain unnoticed herself. He stopped before Hank's Remington sculpture and ran a hand down the horse's flank as she had so often seen Hank do. The men seemed to be fascinated by the piece, and she suspected that both of them regretted the loss of the Old West.

A slight smile curved his mouth, softening the planes of his face. Perhaps he felt as Remington himself had, that "bronze is the thing. Other art forms are a triviality." He looked far more approachable than he had at any other time, except for those dizzying minutes in the vault.

In the week since they had met, Tonia had seen a wide range of emotions on Ben's face, from irritation to passion. Each one made him more interesting to her, and caused her to be very wary. She stood up slowly.

"Hank's not home," she announced. "He had a board of directors meeting at the museum this afternoon, then dinner with friends. He may be back late."

Ben turned in a smooth, easy motion, his smile fading. A quick glance took in Tonia's appearance and settled on her face. For a moment Tonia wondered if he was unsure, considering what approach to take. Then his smile broke out again, and he sauntered toward her.

She watched him, her folded hands resting lightly on the glass case. Her appearance was calm, she hoped.

"I wasn't looking for Hank. I wanted to talk to you."

Her eyes narrowed. "What about?"

Ben's chuckle sent a shiver of pleasure leapfrogging up her spine. "When you look at me like that, I can imagine you plying your Gypsy wares or bargaining in a horse trade. You look sort of shrewd."

"Good. I mean to."

"You think you need to be shrewd to talk to me?"

"Certainly more than I've been since we met."

"As I recall, you've done all right in every encounter." He paused, his eyes taking on a wicked gleam that made him look very much like his uncle. "Except one," he added.

She refused to be baited. "What did you want to talk to me about?"

Ben stepped around the display case to stand beside her. "Do you like your job?"

Tonia edged away. Only a week ago he had tried to bribe her to quit her job. She didn't know the reason behind his question, but she decided to take it at face value. She pretended to be studying the display of old hunting knives she had just rearranged. "Yes. I do."

"You're learning a great deal about law and order in the Old West?" He stepped closer, gazing down at a pearl-handled Bowie knife. "That is what Hank's book is about, isn't it?"

"Yes," Tonia responded, inching away. "Lawmen of the Old West."

"Interesting subject?" Ben's hand trailed along the top of the glass.

"Very."

"Would you like to learn even more about the Old West?" He turned suddenly and pinned her with a gaze.

Tonia started at his sudden movement and bumped into the place where two cases came up together. His nearness had her so rattled she couldn't tell whether he had deliberately backed her into a corner or not.

"Learn more? How?"

An engaging grin lit his face. "Have a drink with me in Old Town."

She blinked. "Old Town was a Spanish settlement. Hardly the Old West."

"It's the best I could do on short notice. If you want authenticity we could drive four hours to the Yuma Territorial Prison but I warn you, the food probably isn't as good."

She shook her head and laughed. "What brought this on?"

"I was sitting at my desk an hour ago when I got a sudden yen...."

"A yen?"

"Don't interrupt. A yen for a margarita. I closed my eyes—" he demonstrated "—and I saw myself sitting at a table at the Bazaar del Mundo." He opened one eye. "However, there was something missing from the picture."

"Someone to pour you into a cab after you finished your drink?" Tonia asked sweetly, beginning to enjoy the game as her caution slipped away.

Ben opened both eyes and gave her a mock glare. "I need a beautiful young woman to complete the picture."

"Where's Chloe?"

"She's too tall and blond. I'm picturing someone with black hair and mysterious brown eyes."

"How about a cocker spaniel?"

"A woman, I said."

"Your secretary?" She started to slip around him.

He blocked her by placing a hip against the edge of the glass case. "Miss Lemmons is bigger than I am and lives up to her name."

"Bad secretary?"

"Good secretary. Bad personality."

Tonia laughed. It wasn't fair. The last time she had seen him, he'd had a half-formed accusation in his eyes. He stayed away for days and now turned up with his disarming grin and line of banter—and she was ready to melt. Still, she couldn't forget that look.

She sobered. "Ben, I want to know if you still think I'm after Hank, or that he's after me. Is this invitation a way of testing me?" She couldn't bring herself to ask if he thought she had taken the bibliography.

"No," he said, the laughter gone from his voice. "Do you think I would invite you out for that reason?"

Tonia lowered her gaze. "I'm not sure, Ben. I don't know you that well."

A very long, painful silence followed in which neither of them spoke. Tonia wanted to go, but it was critical that she know what he thought of her.

"What better way to get to know me than over dinner," he said at last.

"I thought the invitation was just for drinks," she said, all too aware that he hadn't answered her question about Hank.

"Dinner, too."

"I don't know, Ben. I'm tired."

"Then you won't have the energy to cook."

"I'm not dressed to go out." She gestured toward her jeans and loose Mexican top.

"You look fine." Ben's voice took on a teasing tone. "Besides, we can always put a paper bag over your head so no one will recognize you. We'll cut a little hole in the front for the straw."

Tonia's resistance crumpled like so many paper soldiers. She threw up her hands, her eyes sparkling. "You have an answer for everything. All right, I'll go. I'll meet you there so I won't have to come back here for the car."

She started toward Hank's office to get her purse, but Ben followed her.

"I thought your car, uh, died."

"Hank's letting me use one of his cars."

"Which one?"

"The new one."

The pause was a little too long before Ben said, "I see."

Tonia stopped in the doorway and turned quickly, but he was smiling.

"If you want to change clothes, why don't I follow you home, then I'll drive to Micaela's. It will be awkward with two cars, and the parking lots in Old Town aren't that big."

Tonia tipped up her chin. "Are you reluctant to have me drive Hank's car into all that traffic, or are you ashamed to be seen with me in these old jeans?"

Ben closed his eyes briefly. "Listen, Tonia, this isn't going to work if we keep this up. Can't we call a truce? There have been a few pleasant moments when we've been together, haven't there?"

Ashamed, Tonia's eyes wavered from him. "Yes, of course. I *would* like to change clothes, if you don't mind waiting for me."

It was an olive branch, and Ben accepted with a smile. "Lead the way," he invited.

Relieved, Tonia got her purse and headed for Hank's car. The beginning of the drive was rocky because she was so conscious of Ben behind her. He was driving a silver sports car she had seen parked outside Hank's house last Friday.

Having him watch her drive made her nervous. The third time she hit the brakes too hard at a stoplight, she decided she had to calm down. Because of Ralph's peculiarities, she had learned to be a careful driver, but at this rate, she was going to cause an accident.

Mentally, she distracted herself by looking at the familiar scenery in San Diego's Clairemont area as a stranger would. She saw houses, built in the fifties, box-shaped, with roofs that were almost flat. They were homey, though, with yards larger than the more modern ones. The structures had aged gracefully, like their owners, settling into middle age with a complacency that said they'd had enough of small children and noisy pets, and were ready for their quiet senior years.

The Meier's house, white with dark blue trim, had two large olive trees growing in the front yard. They had dropped their black fruit onto the sidewalk, lawn and driveway, leaving oily spots she wished she had cleaned up.

At least the house was neat, she consoled herself. One person didn't make much mess.

As she pulled cautiously into the driveway, Tonia's stomach began fluttering nervously. Should she invite Ben in? It wasn't as if this was a real date, was it? Or was it?

For a moment, Tonia regretted that she hadn't dated in the last couple of years. If she'd had more recent practice, she could carry the situation off with panache.

The house Tonia shared with her mother reflected her own personality more than Annie's. The decor had been chosen with Tonia's love of bright colors in mind. Having Ben see her home seemed like a way to establish herself as someone other than Hank's secretary, a fortune-telling Gypsy, or an hysterical claustrophobic.

She would make the invitation very casual, she decided.

By the time she had stopped the car and emerged to lock it carefully, Ben had walked in from the street to wait for her.

"I would park Hank's car in the garage," she said, frowning at the new vehicle. "But it only holds one car, and it already has—"

"I know," Ben interrupted. "Ralph's body."

Tonia laughed and turned to him with an eager smile. "Would you like to come in?"

So much for casual.

Ben agreed and plucked the house key from her hand to unlock the door. Tonia flipped on lights as she walked in, and dropped her purse on the hall table. "Would you like something to drink while you wait? I think I've got some wine that hasn't been opened more than a few months."

He didn't bother to repress a shudder. "No thanks. I'm fine."

Tonia shrugged and started down the hall to her room. "I won't be long."

"Take your time," Ben answered, his attention already caught by the wall of family photographs and Tonia's collection of animal figurines on the bookcase.

In the bath adjoining her room, Tonia plunged in and out of the shower. She splashed on her favorite scent with a lavish hand, pulled on her underthings and caught her hair back on each side with flashy gold combs. After applying makeup, she slipped into her favorite dress, a slim red creation of such a finely woven synthetic only an expert could tell it from silk. She buckled on her favorite high-heeled sandals and gave herself one last critical inspection in the mirror.

Not bad, she decided, and she had only been twenty minutes from start to finish. She hoped Ben thought it had been worth the wait.

He obviously did, coming forward to clasp her hands in his. His gray eyes were warm as he gazed down at her. "You look lovely. You may want to bring a scarf," he said. "My car doesn't have a top, just a cover that snaps over the seats and steering wheel."

Tonia took a shawl and scarf from the front closet. Ben flipped the front porch light on and locked the door behind them.

"What kind of car is this?" she asked, tucking the folds of her red dress around her and squirming in the hard seat as she tried to get comfortable.

"A Lotus Super Seven." Ben grimaced apologetically at her efforts. "It's built for speed, not comfort."

She watched him pull on driving gloves, fasten his seat belt, including shoulder harness, and prepare to start the engine.

"Oh, that's encouraging," she said dryly.

HE CHUCKLED as they pulled away from the curb. This had been a good idea, he reflected. Seeing her away from Hank's house would help him be more objective about her. She'd been on his mind too much lately.

A few minutes later they were driving toward San Diego's oldest section. Although now a state historical park surrounded by the busy downtown area, Old Town had once been a lonely outpost. It had grown up around the first mission established in California by Father Junipero Serra in 1769. The original mission still stood, restored to serene beauty in its parklike setting overlooking bustling Mission Valley.

At a stoplight on Rosecrans Boulevard, Ben waved a hand in the direction of the mission. "Have you ever been up there?"

When she leaned forward to follow the direction of his gesture, he caught a whiff of her flowery scent. Although faint, the fragrance made him light-headed for a moment.

She wasn't beautiful, he reminded himself, gazing at the creaminess of her skin.

He liked blondes. A blue-black wisp of hair escaped from her scarf and curled beguilingly along her temple.

"To the mission?" she asked, turning her eyes to him.

"Yes. Fourth-grade field trip. That was the year for state history in California."

"I wouldn't know," he answered in a vague tone. "I lived in Michigan until I was ten."

She smiled and settled back against the seat.

Tall women were better, he cautioned. He didn't get a stiff neck bending down to kiss one.

She fit perfectly into the Super Seven's small seat, and she seemed to be enjoying the wind on her face. Most of the women who had ridden in the car complained about its lack of a roof.

Kissing Tonia hadn't been a problem, either, he recalled. She fit perfectly on his lap. That day in the vault—

Ben scowled at the signal light and roared ahead when it turned green.

He had to keep his hands *off* her.

TONIA GLANCED SIDEWAYS at Ben's sudden burst of speed and intent frown. She didn't know what had caused it, but within a few moments he was talking again.

"I hope we can find a parking place near the restaurant. As usual, Old Town's flooded with tourists," he observed, pulling into one of the parking lots. "I don't like to be too far away from the Seven. It wouldn't do much good to lock the doors. Aha!"

He swept into a tiny space near the entrance to Micaela's courtyard and stopped with a smug grin. He helped her out of the low seat and within moments they were seated in view of the outside bar, with oversized margaritas in their hands.

Ben leaned back in the too-small wrought iron chair and looked around. "We shouldn't have to wait long for a table in the dining room. I made our reservations for seven-thirty."

Tonia frowned. "You didn't call from Hank's house. Did you phone from mine?"

Ben looked pleased with himself. "I made the reservations this morning."

"Then all that business about sitting at your desk, et cetera, et cetera wasn't true?"

"No, actually I was playing golf this afternoon," Ben admitted. "But I *did* need a drink."

Tonia was trying to decide whether to laugh or scold when a waiter appeared beside their table. "Are you Mr. Andrews? There's a phone call for you. A Ms Lemmons."

Ben groaned. "That secretary of mine tracks me down
wherever I go. She's got a nose like a bloodhound," he
grumbled as he rose to his feet, settling his hair into place
with his fingers and buttoning his jacket. "Looks like one,
too."

Smiling, Tonia watched him stalk off. This was going to
be easier than she had thought. She could enjoy being with
him as long as she kept her head.

Her gaze followed him as he swung easily around the tables. He was different from the men in her family, who were
dark and barrel-chested. When they walked, they tended to
pound the earth rather than step on it, demanding the world
make a place for them. Her uncle Stephan had always reminded her of a bantam rooster strutting his importance.
Ben, though, had the smooth, easy movements of an ath-
lete. Sitting back in her chair, she sipped her icy drink and
glanced around.

The restaurant's courtyard was busy with the predinner
crowd. Across a low pyracantha hedge that separated the
outdoor tables from the Old Town shops, she caught sight
of a jaunty red plaid beret, and sat up straight when she saw
it belonged to Otis Justin. She jumped up and hurried out
to him.

"Dr. Justin!"

He whirled and stopped. Surprise flashed in his eyes, then
he smiled broadly. "Antonia, I'm so glad to see you."

"I've heard about your shop down here," she said,
looking back the way he had come. "Are you closed for the
day?"

He nodded and told her the hours when The Old Town
Peddler was open. "I just locked up and was going to meet
George and Melvin here for dinner." His glance went to the
restaurant's crowded courtyard. "Maybe we'll have to go
somewhere else," he mused, then looked back at her. "Since

I'm only teaching two classes this semester, I can devote as much time as I want to the shop and my new employees. It's been very profitable." He laughed suddenly. "Very profitable indeed. But I musn't keep you any longer...."

Tonia's smile wavered at his manner. Not exactly nervous, he seemed excited or edgy, anxious to be on his way.

"I just wanted to say hello and thank you again for recommending me for the job with Mr. Tyson. I love it, and I'm learning so much."

"You didn't need my recommendation," Dr. Justin said absently, his fingers fussing with the loose black bow tie he was wearing. "Tyson seemed to know all about you."

"He did?"

"Sure, indicated he only needed a little more information."

"Then how did he hear about me?"

"Didn't say—"

"Otis." At the sound of a low voice from the shadows behind them Tonia jumped and whipped around.

George Heller was wearing dark clothing, and Tonia had to squint to see him in the gathering dusk. He slipped from the shadows of the hedge to join them.

"Evening, Miss Meier. You here to have dinner?" George's dark eyes skimmed over her in a way that made her wish she was still wearing her old jeans and shirt.

"Yes." She shivered and stepped back, disconcerted by him.

"Sometimes there's a long wait in this place."

"Not too much longer," she said coolly. "My date made reservations for seven-thirty." She wasn't sure why she had mentioned Ben except that she wanted to establish she was with someone.

"We don't have reservations, so I guess we'll have to go somewhere else," Dr. Justin said, directing his attention to George. "I'll go tell Melvin to meet us at the van."

George nodded, then said with an air of suppressed excitement, "After we eat, I think Melvin and I'd better go pick up that special order merchandise."

Dr. Justin smiled indulgently at the young man. "You're very conscientious, George. I did right to hire you."

Under his praise, George's eyes took on a sharp gleam.

George and Melvin were obviously a couple of what Tonia called "ugly ducklings," young people with no direction in life for whom Dr. Justin found jobs. She admired the professor's commitment in helping someone like George. Personally, she would never want to spend more than a few minutes in his company—if that.

The professor smiled winningly at Tonia. "It's been a pleasure to see you. Be sure to do some window-shopping while you're here. One of the shops has a display of gold and silver jewelry that would appeal to your Gypsy nature."

She said she would and turned back toward the courtyard. She was almost at the entrance when George spoke.

"Oh, Miss Meier?"

Dr. Justin had started walking away. George was alone.

Tonia's spine grew very stiff, but she managed a frosty smile. "Yes, George?"

His dark eyes lingered on her. One corner of his thin mouth edged upward. "I haven't seen my little sister in a few days. You tell her hi for me, okay?"

Lucy *must* be adopted, Tonia thought. She couldn't possibly be related to this man by blood.

"Certainly. Good night."

"Enjoy your dinner," George's oily voice followed her.

"Thank you." Tonia glanced back. He was strolling after Dr. Justin, and another person slipped from the shadows to join them. When they passed under a streetlight she saw that it was Melvin Morris.

Shaking off the cold feeling his lecherous regard had given her, she returned to the restaurant's courtyard, and almost bumped into Ben who had been watching her approach. He came forward and took hold of her arm. "Where have you been? Who was that guy?"

Still disturbed by her encounter with the two men, and irritated by Ben's sudden possessiveness, Tonia pulled her arm from his grasp. "I'm still here," she said, in a voice that warned him she might not be for long.

He frowned, his gray eyes taking on a stormy darkness. "Our table is ready. Come on." Ben snagged their drinks from the courtyard table and hurried her toward the dining room. A smiling hostess met them and led them to a glass-and-cedar enclosed booth.

The instant the hostess had left Ben turned to her. "Where have you been?"

Consumed with her own quick anger, she didn't hear the gruff concern behind his question. "I don't think I need to make explanations to you."

"Just answer the question."

Tonia perched on the edge of her chair, ready to flee. "I don't have to."

Ben reached across and grabbed her arm.

Oblivious to the scene they were making in the crowded restaurant, Tonia started to shake his hand off, but his grip tightened. She stared at him, willing him to let her go, or show some concern for her, not just rough irritation because he had lost track of her for a moment. "In case you didn't notice, I was on my way *back* to the table when you came running out like a jealous madman."

Their eyes met swiftly, challenging each other. Hers were sparking with righteous indignation, his with anger that faded to irritation then disappeared as suddenly as it had flared. He freed her arm. "Guess I went a little overboard, huh?" He cocked his head toward the courtyard. "That guy you were talking to. I've seen him somewhere. . . ."

Tonia eyed him for a moment before sitting back. Although she hadn't wanted to talk to George in the first place, she found herself having to talk about him. "He was at Hank's party. His name is George—he's Lucy Heller's brother."

"Who?"

"Hank's housekeeper. George works for the man who recommended me to Hank. Dr. Justin's the one I wanted to say hello to."

"You don't have to explain," Ben said, then added on a rueful note, "for all I know you could have been in the ladies' room."

Tonia watched him pluck his glasses from his pocket and begin polishing the lenses, preparatory to putting them on. He had been right earlier. This wasn't going to work if they weren't willing to make enough good moments together to outweigh the bad ones. She leaned forward and took the glasses from him. His gray eyes shot to hers. "Apology accepted," she said gently, winning one of his warmest smiles.

A waiter arrived, and hurriedly they opened their menus and made their selections. When he had written their orders and whisked the menus away, Tonia sat for a moment, sipping her water.

She was amazed at Ben's sudden jealousy, and she suspected he was, too. He had acknowledged his unreasonable response, but she hadn't explained why she was sometimes offended and defensive whenever he demanded explanations from her. If there was going to be anything between them, he had a right to know the reason behind her reaction. She swallowed another drink of water, drew a deep breath and plunged into her explanation.

"I was engaged a couple of years ago—"

Ben's gray eyes riveted on her.

"It didn't last very long. I guess I needed someone to cling to when Mother and I found out how sick my grandfather was. At first I thought Greg was very caring. I soon discovered he was merely possessive. When I wasn't with him, he demanded to know who I was with and what I was doing. He had a very irritating habit of—grabbing my arm and yelling in my face."

"Ouch." Ben winced. "No wonder you weren't too inclined to explain just now. How long did the engagement last?"

"Barely two months."

"Smart girl." Ben applauded. "Tell me, did you read his palm when you first met?"

With a rueful twist of her lips, Tonia shook her head.

He wagged his finger at her. "Let that be a lesson to you."

Their dinner came, and they lingered over their spicy tamales and rice while Ben told her of his plans for more auto-parts stores. The call he had just received from his secretary concerned trouble with his plans to expand into Arizona or New Mexico.

Then, after some prodding, Ben succeeded in getting Tonia to tell him about her family.

"My grandfather, Joe Howard, was a GI in Europe during World War II. He found my mother in a displaced persons camp after the war. He and his wife, Libby, couldn't have children, so they adopted her and brought her to the States. Her family had all died in concentration camps because they were Gypsies—another of Hitler's plans to rid the world of unacceptable people,'' she added, her eyes snapping.

"How old was your mother?"

"Thirteen. Old enough to be entrenched in the Gypsy ways and language. She had never been to school. Couldn't read. Didn't like sleeping indoors or wearing shoes. She says it shows Joe and Libby's determination to civilize her that she graduated only two years behind in high school."

"It must have been hard for her to reconcile the old Gypsy ways with the Yankee work ethic your grandparents probably taught her."

Tonia looked up, pleased that he understood. "It was."

"And your father?"

Tonia sobered and took another bite of her rice. "He was a horse trainer, like many Gypsies. He died when I was six." Her tone was sad, and she wanted to change the subject, but Ben couldn't seem to let it drop.

"Where did your mother meet him? Hadn't she become pretty Americanized?"

"There's a big Gypsy population in California," Tonia said after a moment. "It's just not that visible. After high school mother worked in an office but sought out other Gypsies. Trying to recapture her heritage, I suppose. She only knew my father a short time before they were married. He swept her off her feet."

"What kind of father was he?" Ben asked.

"I don't remember very much." Tonia smiled suddenly. "Except the smell of horses. I think my parents' marriage was pretty tempestuous. Mother sometimes jokes I was the best thing she got out of it."

"Hear, hear."

Tonia warmed to him, marveling at the easy way he had overcome her reluctance to talk about Greg and about her family. When they finished eating they wandered around

Old Town for a while peering in shop windows. Tonia located Dr. Justin's shop and the gold and silver display he had mentioned at another tiny store. She told Ben about the special significance Gypsies attached to gold. To them it was more an adornment than a commodity.

At some point during her explanation, Ben took her hand and stood holding it while he listened. They walked that way as they wandered about the shops. Ben seemed to have forgotten his worries about leaving the Super Seven unattended.

"It's getting late," Ben observed. "I suppose I'd better take you home."

"Yes," she sighed, pulling on her scarf and shawl.

"We both have to work tomorrow."

Tonia ducked her head, smiling. He sounded as reluctant to end the evening as she felt. Despite the rocky start, it had been fun. "Yes, I know."

"Well," he sighed. "Let's go."

At her house, Ben pulled into the driveway behind Hank's car. The neighbor's two German shepherds, who barked at every noise, set up a louder-than-usual racket.

"Sounds like they've got something cornered," Ben commented.

"I hope it's not a skunk. A lot of them come up out of the canyons. I can't tell you how many times Mother and I have jumped out of bed to slam the windows shut."

Ben swallowed. "Uh, what were you wearing when you jumped out of bed?"

Tonia turned and laughed up at him, the full moon falling on her face, making her exotic eyes seem deep with wicked amusement. "None of your business."

"Too bad," Ben lifted his hand suddenly and caught her under the chin. "Do you kiss on the first date?"

Tonia's throat was too tight to answer, so she shook her head.

"Too bad," Ben repeated, then brightened. "Not that you can really consider this a first date. After all, we were locked in the vault together—that has to be considered a first date. Partners in time of trouble or some such thing. Technically we just had our second date. Do you kiss on the second date?"

His fingers were gently rubbing her jaw. His eyes were promising, and the planes and hollows of his lean face were lined in silver by the moon. A smile tilted his lips as he waited for her answer.

"Yes," she whispered and stood on tiptoe.

Ben pulled her into his arms and kissed her deeply. His mouth made all kinds of exotic promises, before he set her away from him. "I don't think Hank's under a Gypsy spell," he said, clearing his throat. He leaned over and rested his forehead against hers so they looked eye to eye. "I think I am."

They drifted toward the front door, their arms about each other.

She wasn't sure if she was glad or disappointed when Ben said, "I'll just see you in, then be on my way." He paused, glancing around. "Hey, wait a minute. Didn't we leave the porch light on?"

"Maybe the bulb burned out," Tonia answered, still drifting on a dreamy cloud of happiness.

Ben grunted agreement, plucking the key from her fingers.

He unlocked the front door and stood back to let Tonia step into the small entryway.

Feeling for the light switch, she stumbled against a small marble-topped table that appeared to be lying on its side. She tried to sidestep it but encountered a toppled wrought iron plant stand. A clay pot that had held a lush fern rolled crazily across the tile floor, strewing dirt.

"What in the—"

Tonia fumbled for the light and finally switched it on. She gave the table at her feet one shocked look before turning to face her living room.

It had been ransacked.

CHAPTER FIVE

HORRIFIED, Tonia surveyed the spilled dirt at her feet. The fern had been ripped out by its long, hairy roots, which stretched out like tentacles.

Her stunned gaze lifted to the scattered contents of her bookcase. Books and animal miniatures were scattered carelessly.

The closet in the entryway stood open. Coats and jackets had been flung to the floor. Her upright vacuum cleaner stood atop the mess, its handle jutting at a crazy angle. As she watched, it overbalanced and toppled with a crash.

She reached out a shaky hand to grasp the open closet door, but Ben grabbed her wrist, then clasped an arm around her waist and whisked her outside.

Tonia struggled against him, her fingers scrabbling to loosen his grip. "My house...."

"Tonia, come on!"

"But I've got to—let go of me! Somebody broke into my house."

"And they may still be in there." Ben pulled her down the walk. "If they didn't hear us come in and turn on the light, they heard that vacuum cleaner fall over. Come on, I want you to go to a neighbor's and call the police."

Confused and frightened, she stumbled along with him. "But what are you—"

Ben touched his fingers to her lips. "Keep your voice down. While you place the call, I'll check around inside."

"Are you crazy?" she whispered fiercely. "You just said they might still be in there."

"And if they are, I'll hold them for the police."

She turned back toward her own front door. "I'm coming with you!"

He grabbed her shoulders and whirled her around. "No! Now get along, we're wasting time!"

Before she could argue further, Ben gave her a quick, savage kiss and sent Tonia next door where Mr. Ford let her in to use the phone. Ben joined her there in a few minutes to report that the house was empty and only the living room and dining area had been vandalized.

Two hours later the police had come and gone after telling Ben and Tonia that the intruders probably had fled when they heard someone coming home. They had gone out the back door, which they seemed to have opened easily with a thin-bladed knife or screwdriver.

Nothing appeared to be missing. Tonia had mentioned the barking dogs down the street, and the officers left to question the owners.

When they were alone, Tonia and Ben put the living room to rights. She got out the furniture polish and removed every trace of fingerprint powder left by the police and, she hoped, every trace of the vandals. She set her miniatures up in their precise order once again. Miraculously, none of them were broken. Ben went into the kitchen to make tea.

Tonia rubbed at everything she thought the intruders might have touched. She was going over the front of the bookcase for the third time when Ben came back and set two mugs of tea on the coffee table. He watched Tonia's frantic motions for several moments, then he walked up behind her and gently took the dust rag from her hand.

"Come have some tea. It'll help you calm down."

"I don't want to calm down. I want to finish this." She grabbed for the rag, but he tossed it onto a shelf.

"Don't argue. Sit down."

She gave him a killing look, stalked toward the couch, flopped down and grabbed the cup. She took a mouthful of the scalding brew and almost spewed it back into the cup.

Stupid, she thought, pressing the back of her hand to her tender mouth and squeezing her eyes shut against threatening tears. Being vulnerable made her overreact.

"Hey, are you all right?"

"No," she snapped, allowing tears to fill her eyes. "I'm furious. I feel violated. No one has the right to come into my house and tear it up."

"That's exactly what the law says," Ben pointed out harshly. "And I hope the law gets the chance to deal with them."

"And if they don't?" she snorted.

"Here." Ben pushed the mugs back on the coffee table, scooped her up and sat her on his lap. "This is getting to be a habit with me," he said, forcing her to lean against him.

"Don't do me any favors."

"I'm not." Ben snuggled her against him and rested his chin on the top of her head. He forced her arms to clasp his waist. "I'm testing a theory."

"A theory?"

"I have several female employees, and I've had opportunities to watch them face trouble. They're all different."

"How?" In spite of herself, Tonia was interested. She let her tense muscles relax a little as Ben's hand came up under her hair and began massaging her neck. His fingers rubbed the knotted muscles, beginning to ease out the tension.

"Some fall to pieces, have hysterics," he said. "Some turn grim. The others get mad as hell and then..."

"And then what?" Tonia lifted her head to look at him.

His eyes, only millimeters away, were sympathetic and lit with a hint of mischief. "Then—they get even."

Her soft laugh was rueful. "That's exactly how I feel!"

"Maybe you'll get your chance." Ben's fingers continued to massage her neck until the tightness loosened, but his expression fell into hard lines. "If I have anything to do with it," he vowed.

Comforted, her fury began to fade but left a bitter sense of outrage. She knew that in a day or so she could look at the incident more rationally. Ben could be right. She might get a chance to find out who had violated her house and, with Ben's help, she would make sure they were prosecuted.

Tonia tilted her head back to look at him. This close, she could see the fine lines that rayed out from the corners of his gray eyes. His sculptured features were softened by the glow of the table lamp beside them. Remembering how he had kissed her that day in the vault and earlier this evening, her eyes went to his lips and then back up to meet his gaze.

"Ben, why are you here? Why did you stay? You could have left when the police did."

"Do you want me to go?"

"No."

"Then what *do* you want?" He didn't need to ask the question. He could read the answer in her eyes.

"For you to kiss me."

He touched his lips to her cheek. A riot of sensations overwhelmed him. He could smell the perfume that had faded during the evening. Once again, the honeysuckle seemed out of place to him, incongruous with her exotically slanted eyes, dark with mystery. But the scent suited her personality, sweet and fresh, unpretentious.

Tonia rested her face against his mouth, her heart's pace accelerating with her breathing. She felt safe with Ben.

Maybe that was a mistake, but she didn't want to explore the negatives right now. She made a vaguely dissatisfied sound. "More, Ben."

His breath caught. "Tonia...."

"Please."

He could have resisted a demanding woman, bent on her own satisfaction. A quip and a disarming smile would have defused the situation, but the need Tonia was showing was more than he could resist.

He moved his lips in a slow glide across her cheek and nibbled at the corner of her mouth. "This?"

"Mmmm."

With a bemused chuckle, he touched his mouth to hers.

Tonia melted into him, letting the first instant of pure pleasure run its course before she began to need more, kissing him with a fervor that he returned.

Finally, breathing raggedly, he pulled away and turned his face from hers.

Tonia could feel his heart pounding against her ear, and she smiled, knowing he was as affected as she was.

Her befuddled brain tried to sort out the series of events that had brought her to this point. Ben had been catapulted into her life by his uncle's practical joke, and now he was comforting her after an attempted robbery. She lowered her head and shook it, marveling at the strange turn of events.

Ben tucked his chin and looked down at her. "What's the matter?"

"I was thinking about the day we met and everything else that's happened."

Her smile, and the smoldering look she was giving him were an invitation. Ben knew it. He also knew she was feeling grateful to him, but she was too vulnerable right now for what she obviously had in mind.

He was very solemn. "Tonia, something more is going to happen if we keep this up. Are you ready for it?"

Tonia's face pinkened. If she had thought at all about making love with him, it was with the hope that he would take the decision out of her hands. He wouldn't. Ben was too honest not to have her full consent and cooperation.

She let her hair fall forward, hiding her face. "No," she admitted, "but if I asked you to, would you?"

"In a heartbeat, but not now," he said with gentle gruffness. "Your house has already been violated. I'm not going to do the same to your body."

With an embarrassed laugh, she scooted off him to stand beside the sofa. It hadn't been a rebuff, and she didn't feel hurt.

"Is there someone who can come over and spend the night with you? Besides me, that is."

"Yes. If you'll wait while I call her."

THE SHYLY HOPEFUL LOOK Tonia cast Ben almost made him forget his resolve to give her time. He would have made a grab for her if she hadn't turned suddenly and gone into the kitchen. Ben passed an unsteady hand through his hair and headed for the back of the house where he checked all the window locks.

He finished up in a bedroom with brightly flowered fabric walls and matching bedspread. He knew it was Tonia's. The outrageous colors evinced the vitality of her nature, while a shelf of dolls over her bed captured her humor and whimsy.

Ben couldn't believe how the thought of her being in danger had shaken him. Just as seeing her with that guy at Old Town had shaken him. What was his name? Helmer? Heller. Ben took his glasses out of his jacket pocket and chewed on the earpiece for a moment before slipping them on.

Her reaction to his kiss, although he knew it sprang from her vulnerability, had nearly driven him over the edge. If she had said she was ready—if he had thought she was ready—nothing would have stopped him from staying.

He was deeply grateful she hadn't been home when the vandals had mindlessly trashed her home—and he was terrified of how much he cared. Unready to feel that deeply, he needed some distance. Casting an unwilling look of longing at her bed, he left the room and went into the kitchen where he checked the lock and shoved a chair under the knob of the back door.

TONIA HAD TELEPHONED her best friend, Maria Cortez, who threw a few things into a bag and rushed over.

"Why didn't you call me right away?" she scolded, hugging Tonia and glancing around the room for evidence of the crime.

Maria watched wide-eyed as Tonia saw Ben out the door. He gave her a brief hug, pulling her against him with one arm. The gesture was friendly and comforting, right for the moment. She couldn't help feeling disappointed, though, that he didn't kiss her. As he walked out the door, he seemed very remote, but she attributed it to Maria's presence. Ben wouldn't want to embarrass her.

As soon as the door closed behind him, Maria demanded to know all about Ben, their evening together and what the police officers had said. Tonia poured out the now cold tea Ben had made and brewed a fresh pot. They chatted until Tonia was too tired to be nervous.

Once she was in bed, though, with Maria sleeping in her mother's room, Tonia's mind replayed the scene on the couch. She was grateful now that he hadn't taken what she offered. He had known she sought comfort, not love.

Since they had met, Tonia had regarded Ben with a confusing mixture of attraction, irritation and bemusement. Because she had read his palm, she knew what motivated him. She had been disarmed by his concern for Hank and by the way he'd comforted her when she was upset. He didn't hesitate to show her that he found her attractive.

Most of all, he had charmed her, making her forget the barriers she had put up to keep men at arm's length for the last two years. She felt, at last, that she could trust one. She was ready for Ben Andrews.

"WE'RE GETTING YOU A DOG," Hank said when she arrived at his house the next morning. "A big, mean dog!"

Surprised, Tonia allowed him to pull her in the front door and give her a rough hug. "Why didn't you call me? Ben had to call and tell me all about it. I don't like this at all," he went on, hustling her into the living room and handing her a cup of coffee as though she had just gone through a life-shattering ordeal. He sat down beside her and patted her knee awkwardly. "First you get locked in the vault when you're scared of little places, and now your house has been broken into by a bunch of punks."

"Well, apparently that's all it was. A police officer called this morning and said they couldn't find any evidence to identify the burglars." She frowned. It infuriated her that the intruders couldn't be found immediately. She wanted them punished. "He thinks it might be a bunch of teenage vandals who've hit several places in the city."

She was about to go on when she was struck by something Hank had just said. "How did you know I had claustrophobia? I never mentioned it, did I?"

Hank looked nonplussed for a moment. She could have sworn he blushed, if crusty old men could be said to blush. "You didn't have to," he said. "I could tell by the way you avoided the vault."

"Oh," she said, unconvinced. Then she was struck by another thought that had been nagging her. "By the way, I saw Dr. Justin last night in Old Town."

"Who?"

"You know, the man who recommended me for this job—only apparently he didn't really do so. Hank, how did you get my name?"

"Oh, here and there..." he answered coyly. "Now don't change the subject. We're getting a locksmith out to your house to put on better locks, and then I'll call the guy from the electronics firm that put the security system in this place to do one in yours. Then we'll start calling kennels."

Tonia's mind reeled at these plans. She could see her paychecks being eaten up for the rest of her life. "Hank, I can't afford all that," she said weakly.

"It's a gift. What's the point of me having all this money if I can't spend it on whatever I want?"

She bridled, clapping her coffee cup down on the table before the sofa. "A gift? It's too much!"

"Damned Yankee Gypsy pride," he muttered. "I've dealt with your type before. All right then, it'll be a loan. Two percent interest. Payments start whenever you want."

"Hank...."

"You want your mother to come home to what you did last night?"

He had her there. Facing a vandalized house, even with Ben beside her, had been horrible. She couldn't handle the thought of her mother doing the same.

She agreed to Hank's plans, and he went off to make phone calls with triumph gleaming in his eyes. Tonia started to work, ruing the day she had become involved with the men in this family. But, one way or another, she couldn't resist them!

Tonia expected to hear from Ben all day, but she understood that he probably couldn't call if he was busy at the office. He had told her some snags had come up in his Arizona deal. Besides, if he had spent the previous afternoon on the golf course, he would have a lot of work to catch up on. She prepared a speech to thank him again for helping her out the previous night, planning to very subtly let him know that she was ready for their relationship to become more serious.

If he called, she was going to ask him over for dinner. She wasn't a great cook, but there were one or two meals she could manage pretty well...

Ben did call in the late afternoon to see how she was, and she prattled on for several minutes about Hank's plans for protecting her home, but when Ben remained unnaturally silent, her words stumbled to a halt.

She twisted her fingers in the phone cord. "Is something wrong, Ben?"

"No." He sounded as remote as he had looked the night before when he left her house. "But I've got to go out of town for a few days. Business."

"Oh." Tonia's thoughts scrambled, and she tried to realign them. He sounded so odd. "Well, have a safe trip, then."

"Yeah. Maybe I'll try to call again," he said. Then he added gruffly, "Take care of yourself, Tonia."

"All right." Considering his sudden coolness, Tonia wished she could disguise the hope that vibrated in her tone.

When Ben hung up, she sat staring at the receiver until the loud beeping jerked her out of her reverie. What had she done or said that had made him so remote?

Saturday evening Tonia was drying her hair when she thought she heard the phone ringing. She switched off the blow dryer's high-pitched whine. When the phone rang again, she lunged for it.

She caught up the receiver on the next ring and heard the faint crackle that told her it was a long-distance call.

"Hello."

"Antonia. Is something wrong?"

"Hello, *Mamio*. No, nothing's wrong." Tonia barely managed to swallow her disappointment. She sat down on the edge of the bed and tightened the belt on her robe.

"You sound out of breath."

"I was drying my hair. I was afraid the phone would stop ringing before I got here."

"Well, I would have called back."

But I didn't think it was you, Tonia said silently. And Ben might not call back. "I'm here now. How are you?"

"I'm all right," Annie Meier said offhandedly. "My *shey*, I've tried to call you several times in the last couple of days. Is everything okay?"

"Fine. I've just been busy. I've been working late, and Hank and I have been out looking for a dog."

"He's buying a dog?"

Tonia smiled at the disapproval in her mother's tone. Annie didn't care for dogs unless they had a useful purpose. Hunting, police and Seeing Eye dogs were the only ones she considered worthy. Tonia suspected it was because as a child Annie's family had owned a pack of mongrels that followed their Gypsy caravan. The mutts shared what little the family had and didn't pay their way.

"For me, actually. He thinks you and I might need some protection."

"From what?"

Too late, Tonia bit her lip. She hadn't meant to give her
mother even a hint about the break-in. Since nothing had
been taken, she saw no reason to alarm her mother need-
lessly. Annie would cut her vacation short and hurry home
if she thought Tonia was in danger.

"Oh, just in case," Tonia said lamely. "Hank worries
about me here alone."

The alarm in Annie's voice melted. "Oh, really?" she
cooed. "How sweet of him."

Tonia held the receiver away and looked at it. Sweet?
"Uh, well, he's a good boss...."

"The best you've ever had."

"Well, yes."

"Then the dog idea is all right with me, since I won't be,
uh, home for a while. You can housebreak it before I get
back. Now," she went on briskly, "what else has been happening? How is Hank's book coming?"

They chatted for several minutes, and Tonia hung up,
smiling at the effervescence in her mother's tone. The cruise
and the stay in Mexico were doing her mother a world of
good. She returned to the bathroom, thinking once again of
Ben, sure he would call soon.

By Sunday afternoon, she realized he wasn't going to call.

At first she was hurt, then puzzled that he wasn't more
concerned about her welfare.

By slow degrees she became angry, especially after Hank
told her early the next week that Ben had phoned him several times and asked about her before flying to Phoenix on
business. She decided that the next time Ben showed up at
Hank's house, with his engaging grin and winning line of
banter, she would ignore him.

Now, if he would just come, so that she could!

She knew her indignation was justified, but she wondered if her reaction to him had driven him away. She had

all but begged him to make love to her. Maybe he had been repelled by her forwardness, and inwardly she writhed with embarrassment, sure this was the case, the reason he'd sounded so distant on the phone.

Between her regular work, dealing with locksmiths and security systems men and visiting what seemed like every kennel in the county with Hank, Tonia had little time to brood about Ben's defection.

As the days passed, with her so involved in her own problems, she didn't notice that Lucy, always quiet, had become more withdrawn, going about her housework at Hank's hardly speaking.

One afternoon Tonia walked into the kitchen for a glass of iced tea. Lucy was sitting at the table with Melvin, her boyfriend, who was leaning across the table, talking earnestly to her. The girl was frowning and had started to speak just as Tonia pushed the door open.

Sensing she had interrupted something important, Tonia hesitated in the doorway. Lucy dropped her gaze, picked up a paper napkin and began to rub at an imaginary spot on the table. Melvin leaped to his feet, his head bobbing. "Hello, Miss Meier."

Tonia almost giggled at his obvious embarrassment. She knew that the two of them hadn't been doing anything illicit, but Melvin certainly looked guilty.

Maybe Hank had told Lucy not to spend time visiting during working hours. But she couldn't imagine that, since Hank was the most lenient of employers and Lucy seldom took a break at all. She seemed always to be working—cooking, cleaning, serving coffee or beer to Hank's frequent visitors.

"Hello, Melvin," Tonia answered, feeling disconcerted by the way he was staring at her. "Lucy, excuse me, but is there any iced tea?"

The girl hurried to wait on Tonia despite her protest that she could serve herself. There was a tension in the room that Tonia couldn't quite define. She felt as though the two of them had been arguing, and wondered if their romance was breaking up.

At that moment she realized how withdrawn Lucy had been lately. She berated herself for having been so wrapped up in thoughts of Ben. Lucy could have used someone to listen. Making a mental note to catch Lucy alone later, she took the proffered drink and escaped the uneasy atmosphere of the kitchen.

ALTHOUGH HANK HAD MENTIONED his upcoming fishing trip, Tonia had forgotten the date, and it came as a surprise when he announced on Thursday that she could have Friday off because he would be gone.

"But Hank, there's a lot I could do here, even though you'll be gone."

"No, the house will be all locked up. I don't really want you here alone."

Tonia drew herself up, trying to hide her hurt, but Hank noticed it.

"Now, don't get your face screwed on sideways," he said gruffly. "I'd trust you with anything I have, even my Remington horse," he added with a magnanimous gesture toward the bronze statue. "I think you need some time off. Things haven't been all that easy on you lately, what with having those punks vandalize your house, and you breaking your heart over that young fool."

Tonia's eyes widened as her face flushed pink. Had she been that obvious? No wonder Ben hadn't called all week if she'd looked at him like a lovesick calf. "You mean Ben?"

"Yeah." Hank's eyes gleamed for a moment. "Now don't look like somebody just found out your best-kept secret. I've been in love myself, and I know all the signs."

"You're reading the wrong signs," she said. "I'm not likely to fall in love with a man who seems to care what happens to me one day and disappears the next."

"He's scared."

"Of me?"

"Of getting serious."

"I didn't ask him to!"

"You don't have to. There's something about a woman like you, kind of casual and—what's the word? Earthy, yeah, that's it. Makes a man start thinking about settling down. Believe me, I know." Before she could protest, Hank went on. "That's why I think you should take an extra day off, think about things. Decide if you want someone like Ben...."

"I don't! And I don't want you to play matchmaker. That's what you were doing the night of your party, wasn't it? Telling me all about Ben's old flame...."

"All right, all right." Hank held his hands up in the air. "I just thought I'd give Cupid a little push."

Tonia sighed. "Please stop it. If you want me to take the day off, I will—" She stopped, a look of consternation passing over her face, and sighed. "You know it's very clever the way you do that."

"What?"

"As if you didn't know. First, you start off talking about something you know I don't want to do, like take extra time off when there's work here to be done. Then you switch to a subject I don't want to talk about—"

"Like my bullheaded nephew?"

"Yes. Then we end up at the original subject and you get me to agree to what you wanted in the first place!" Tonia placed her hands on her hips and looked at him in fond exasperation. "Honestly, my mother does the very same thing. You're two of a kind."

Hank laughed, his blue eyes sparkling. "Well, what do you think of that."

TONIA DECIDED that if Hank was going to give her an extra day off she would spend it cleaning house. She had been spot cleaning things all week. In the middle of a task, such as cooking breakfast, she would think of an item or piece of furniture the intruders might have touched, grab her cleanser and rag and go after the offending area.

If asked, she couldn't have said if it was due to her restlessness and fear after the break-in or the ancient rules of cleanliness the Gypsies maintained. Important events in life—birth, marriage, death—were preceded and followed by ritualistic cleaning. A new mother couldn't fix her family's meals for several weeks after a baby's birth. Illnesses were cured with herbal elixirs and therapeutic baths. Contagious people were separated from the Gypsy band until they could prove they were cured.

What her own momentous occasion was, Tonia couldn't pinpoint. She refused to consider what Hank had said—she couldn't be in love with Ben. His alternating affection and defection hurt too much, especially after she had realized she could become serious about him. For better or worse, she knew the reasons for Ben's uncertainty and vowed never again to get involved with a man whose palm she had read.

Her mind went to Greg. She wouldn't get involved with a man whose palm she *hadn't* read, either.

Friday night brought the last of the winter rains. Tonia picked up Hank's cleaned and repaired books at the bindery and drove home through the snail-paced evening traffic.

She stored the books in her front closet and spent the evening planning her cleaning attack on the house.

Next day the customary San Diego fog cleared off early, leaving a bright, crisp morning. Tonia bounced out of bed and pulled on a pair of jeans and her oldest sweatshirt. She swept her hair into a ponytail with a big clip, and started toward the kitchen to fix breakfast.

When the doorbell rang, she detoured toward it with a smile, expecting it to be her friend, Maria, ready for their usual Saturday morning coffee.

It was Ben.

For a moment Tonia felt as though all the air had been pulled from her lungs. He, too, was dressed casually in jeans, but his were teamed with a sports shirt and a sky-blue pullover sweater. He looked handsome, endearing—and very uncomfortable. She drew in a quick breath and tried for her coolest look.

"Yes?"

"Hi. I was just in the neighborhood and thought I'd drop by."

She gave that statement the attention it deserved by starting to shut the door in his face. His foot was quicker.

"I wanted to see how you were."

"You could have called and asked me a week ago."

He stuck his hands in his pockets and leaned against the doorframe. He glanced up the street to where one of her elderly neighbors was washing his car, then he looked back at her, but his eyes didn't quite meet hers when he said, "Yeah, I know."

"But you didn't," Tonia said, the week's frustration boiling in her. "So don't show up here expecting—" one hand flew wide in an impatient gesture "—I-don't-know-what. You act concerned about me, you phone once, give me the brush-off, then you disappear. I'm just not going to play that game."

"I *was* concerned," he said firmly. "I called Hank every day to ask about you."

She rolled her eyes. "If secondhand information is what you want, fine. You just keep asking him. But don't try to see me."

Once again she tried to shut the door in his face, but this time he wedged his whole upper body in the doorway. "Listen to me, Tonia. I didn't call because..."

"Well?"

"I didn't call because—oh hell," he groaned. "I've got this sick feeling you're the kind of woman a man could fall in love with."

CHAPTER SIX

"TONIA, I didn't mean that the way it sounded."

Ben's voice was muffled. Tonia had given him a shove in the middle of his chest and slammed the door on him, nearly pinching his nose.

"Go away!"

"Not until you let me explain."

"I don't want to hear it."

"Tonia, you're being childish. Just open the door and let me talk to you. I promise, if you don't like my explanation, I'll go away and leave you alone!"

"No!"

"It's pretty early," he observed, rattling the knob loudly. "I wonder if your neighbors are ready to wake up."

She whirled and jerked the door open. "Don't you dare! Everyone is nervous since the break-in here last week." She paused. "On second thought, go ahead." She nodded in the direction of the neighbor who was washing his car. "I could ask him to turn the hose on you, and I saw another neighbor cleaning his shotgun yesterday."

Ben's angry tone dropped away. "You wouldn't let your neighbor shoot me, would you?"

One of Tonia's dark brows rose.

"Forget that question. Tonia, just give me five minutes."

She considered him. On one hand she was furious that he hadn't called all week. On the other hand, she wanted to hear what he had to say. "Can you guarantee that you will take only five minutes?"

"Is there a timer on your watch?" he asked, glancing down at the Swatch watch on her wrist. "If I'm not finished in time, you can kick me out."

She leveled a look at him. It told him she didn't believe in his willingness to accept her terms. "I have a kitchen timer."

Ben bit his lip, looking as if he was trying not to smile. "Whatever you say."

She gave a curt nod. "Five minutes."

Tonia stepped back for him to come in. An invitation, but not a gracious one.

Ben watched her shut the door, then ran his hand around the back of his neck. "I suppose it would be pushing things to ask for a cup of coffee?"

She seared him with a look.

"Yeah, I thought so."

"Please get to the reason for your visit. You're wasting the five minutes."

"Thanks," he said, starting into the living room. "I *will* have a seat."

Tonia's gaze wavered from him. She had meant to be firm, not rude. Now that she looked at him more closely, she realized he could use a cup of coffee. His face was drawn, and his eyes were as dark and troubled as storm clouds.

"I'll go set the kitchen timer," she said, turning away as she felt her determination being undermined by the turmoil in Ben's face.

Involuntarily, she glanced back to see him sink onto the couch and extend his feet in front of him. He leaned his head against the brightly upholstered cushions and closed his eyes. The dazzling print made his face look even more ashen.

In the kitchen she set up the coffee maker and stood watching the dark brew drip into the carafe, unconcerned that Ben's five minutes had long since passed. Whatever the reason for Ben's absence the past week, despite the crazy thing he had just blurted, Tonia was shaken to see his distress. The depth of her feeling for him had been revealed the instant he slumped onto her sofa, as if he was struggling with a decision that centered on her. As well as being flattered, Tonia was frightened.

In the living room, Ben looked up with a relieved smile when she handed him a coffee mug. "I'll take this as a good sign. You remembered I drink it black."

She perched on the edge of a wing chair opposite him and waited, her head tilted to one side.

Leaning forward, Ben rested his forearms on his knees and stared into his mug. "I called Hank every day this week to see how you were. I had to go to Phoenix and Tucson. It looks like my plans for expansion will have to be put on hold."

When he paused, Tonia wondered if that was all he was going to say. She was amazed at the tension in his voice.

"The supplier I had lined up was forced to back out of the deal. Problems with their parent company.... They said maybe in the near future, but I've already got someone scouting new locations. I don't know how long I can wait—but you don't want to hear all this." He sighed. "I'm babbling."

She couldn't have agreed more.

Ben sipped his coffee and set the mug down, being careful to place it exactly in the center of a coaster. "I never considered myself to be a coward," he went on, "but I guess I am. Last week, it scared the hell out of me that you might be in danger, and that I cared what happened to you."

In an instant Tonia's lingering anger faded, to be replaced with wonder. So, Hank had been right.

He looked very uncomfortable. If he'd been wearing a tie he would have been tugging at it.

"You see, Tonia," he went on. "There was a woman I loved a long time ago.... I was...hurt when she married someone else. I don't know if what I feel for you is love or not. I wasn't even looking for a relationship...." Ben shook his head and ran his fingers through his hair. "This is sounding worse and worse."

"Ben—"

"Let me finish," he said, holding up his hand, "before I change my mind."

Tonia eased back, prepared to give him time.

After a moment he went on. "Hank's been parading women in front of me for years, hoping I'd be interested in one. Funny, I wasn't even suspicious about you—not in that way. I thought you were after him—the old lech."

"I'm not responsible for Hank's practical jokes or his manipulations—"

Ben held up his hand again. "I know that. That's not why I stayed away this week. I had to sort out my feelings about you. The trip to Arizona was...convenient."

Tonia was now vacillating between humor and disbelief. She didn't know whether to hug him or slug him. "And did you sort out your feelings?"

He shrugged. "No."

Tonia lifted her hands, palms upward, and let them drop into her lap. "Then why are you here?"

"I was wondering if you would spend the day with me."

"You've got to be kidding!"

"Tonia, how much time have we spent alone together? A few minutes on the beach...on Hank's terrace...locked in a vault. One date in a crowded restaurant and afterward cleaning up your vandalized house. That's not enough to build on." He paused, his gray eyes searching her face. "Just one day, suspending all doubts."

"You asked me that once before, the night we went to Old Town."

"Yes, I did."

"Then you disappeared for a week."

"Yes, I did," he repeated, then grimaced ruefully. "I must seem like a real jerk! But as you said, I am the type who would fall in love for life. That's not something to be entered into lightly. I've got to be sure."

Tonia clasped her hands against her stomach. She had to be sure, too. For a moment she had the dizzying feeling she was teetering on a precipice. She stood and prowled about the room.

"And *you've* got to be sure," Ben continued.

Tonia's determination wavered. Perhaps he was right. She had probably been expecting more from their time together than he had. Now he was ready to go a step farther—and she was hesitating.

"This is crazy."

"Spend the day with me anyway."

"Thereby adding to the confusion," Tonia said dryly.

"The pleasure." He smiled. The tension began to ease from his face. "You'll add to *my* pleasure."

She eyed the appealing grin that always seemed to get to her. She respected his honesty. Her feelings were just as confused as his, but at least he admitted it. Maybe spending the day with him would help her sort things out, too. By the end of the day they might either love each other or lose interest. Either thought scared her to death.

"All right," she finally said, winning a wide grin from him. "But I must be crazy."

Leaving him to finish his coffee, she went to change into a pair of white slacks and a striped top of persimmon orange. After slipping on neon-hued sneakers and grabbing a scarf, she met him at the front door with a wry smile.

"Second thoughts?" Ben asked.

"Yes."

"Serious ones?"

"This may lead nowhere. Are you prepared for that?"

"This may lead everywhere. Are *you* prepared for that? Come on, there's something I want to show you."

Outside he helped her into a different car than the one he had driven the night they went to Old Town, a shiny black Jensen Healy. It was a small, sporty hatchback. Unlike most sports cars, it had a back seat. Inside and out, it looked as if it was in perfect condition.

Ben told her that the vintage car was a limited edition that he had managed to buy from the original owner. Listening to him, Tonia relaxed, enjoying being with him.

They drove to a garage near his office building where he showed her the rest of his car collection. Besides the Jensen and the Super Seven, he owned what he called the oldest living Alfa Romeo and an incredibly beat-up Rolls Royce. Buying classic old cars and restoring them was his hobby.

Tonia admired the big luxury Rolls. Running her hand over a series of small round holes in one of its doors, she asked, "Who was the original owner of this car—Al Capone?"

Ben looked insulted. "That's where I took some trim off to have it rechromed. These aren't bullet holes."

She gave him a saucy grin and moved over to the Alfa Romeo. He unlocked it for her proudly and held the door open.

"Considering the way the men in your family love to collect things, I hope your assortment of cars doesn't grow as big as Hank's assortment of Western memorabilia,'' she teased, sitting in the driver's seat and running her hands around the steering wheel.

Ben stood between the opened door and the car and watched her pleasure in his prize. "I hope not, too. We might have a storage problem.''

When she finished admiring his cars, he held out his hand for hers. "Come on, let's go be crazy.''

In the Jensen again, Tonia asked, "Where are we going?''

"Downtown.''

"Downtown takes in a lot of territory.''

"Horton Plaza.''

Her eyes lit up. "Ohhh—the cupcake.''

"The what?''

"That's what it looks like to me. A cupcake frosted in pink, mauve and yellow.''

"Woman, you've really got a lot of class,'' he jeered good-naturedly, maneuvering the car around a cement truck. "I'll have you know Horton Plaza is a startling marriage of the best in classic and modern architecture. Built on the site of a town square established by the founder of modern San Diego, A. E. Horton, the plaza was designed by one of America's foremost architects and has brought renewed economic life to the downtown area. In a sense it is the jewel in the downtown redevelopment crown.''

Tonia pretended to be dozing in her seat.

Ben poked her in the ribs. "Am I boring you?''

"I don't know,'' she mumbled. "Are my eyes glazed over?''

He gave her a careful look. "Yes.''

"You're boring me.'' She sighed. "You really know how to show a girl a good time.''

"I was trying to educate you.''

"You talk like a retailer.''

"I *am* a retailer."

Tonia collapsed into giggles.

Still, she was bothered by the niggling feeling that she had missed a few steps in their stop-and-go relationship, but she had promised herself she would enjoy the moments with him and not think about problems.

As they neared Horton Plaza, Ben said it looked more like a wedding cake than a cupcake. Its pastel levels were connected with arched walkways, open sidewalks and escalators. Visitors wouldn't have been surprised to see a giant bride and groom on the highest tier.

Ben and Tonia ambled through the shops, admiring the merchandise. At Abercrombie & Fitch, Ben bought a deer-stalker cap and a pipe. Tonia told him he looked more like Steve Martin than Sherlock Holmes, and he retaliated by going upstairs to a toy store and buying her a four-foot-tall Godzilla. He had it blown up and then led her, laughing helplessly, down to a photographer who took their picture with the toothsome green creature.

They left the plaza with Godzilla stuffed sideways in the Jensen Healy's back seat. His head was plastered up against the back window.

"Where are we going now?" Tonia asked, reaching back to shove the monster's bottom back onto the seat. She made an exasperated sound. "Your new son is trying to climb into the front seat."

"I don't believe in sparing the rod," he said pedantically. "Besides, all children in my family must wear seat belts in the car."

Laughing, Tonia twisted around, slapped Godzilla's bottom back into place, and fastened the lap belt. "Now," she said, settling back into her seat. "Where are we going?"

"The public library."

"ning on paying a fine?"

"We're going to leave an immortal message to ourselves."

"Immoral? Could we get arrested for this?"

"Immortal," Ben said, stretching out the word and stressing the T.

"I can't wait."

Inside the big building, they wrote a message, stuck it into the R volume of the Encyclopedia Britannica and vowed to return the next year on the same date to see if it would still be there.

On their way out, Tonia skidded to a halt before a display of rare and valuable books.

"Oh," she cooed, crouching down before the case. "Wouldn't Hank love these?"

"Only if they deal with the West."

"No, these seem to be a pretty mixed bag." She squinted at the tiny card on a volume bound in cracked and peeling leather. "This one is a first edition of Dickens's *A Tale of Two Cities*. It must be worth a fortune."

She glanced at the other volumes. One was a history of sixteenth-century Europe. Thinking of the wealth of information it might contain about the Gypsy migration through that continent, she half whispered fervently, "I'd give *anything* to own a book like that."

She glanced up to see Ben frowning at the glass case. "Yes," he said slowly. "These are worth a lot, all right."

A frisson of disquiet touched Tonia's spine and she shivered.

Ben's eyes snapped to her. "Are you cold? Let's get back out in the sun."

Their next stop was Seaport Village where they visited the shops and watched the sailboats on the bay. Noon found them wandering along the sidewalk munching n

By midafternoon they were in Balboa Park's Museum of Man.

"Who's better looking?" Ben stood beside Cro-Magnon man, posing like a muscle man at the beach.

Tonia walked around, rubbing her chin and peering at him like an art connoisseur. "Well, speaking strictly as an expert on troglodytes and pithecanthropi..."

"Watch it," Ben warned. "Your anthropology classes are showing."

"He's better looking," she finally announced. "You aren't hairy enough." She skipped away before Ben could catch her.

During the day they talked about whatever came to mind. Tonia learned that Ben liked spicy foods. She promised to make *sarmi* for him sometime, a highly seasoned Gypsy dish of pork, rice and tomatoes.

When shadows began stretching dark fingers across the park's pathways they started back toward Ben's car. His arm was around her shoulders, Tonia's around his waist. Their steps slowed as they came close to the Jensen, both of them sensing that their perfect day was over. They were pleasantly tired and cheerfully rumpled. Tonia's hair was tumbling out of its clip and she had nacho sauce on her shirt. Ben's pants sported grass-stained knees.

"Are you hungry?"

"Ben! After all those nachos, a frozen fruit bar and about two gallons of popcorn? Don't tell me *you* are."

"No, thirsty."

"Let's go to my house. I'll make *chao*."

"I thought that was Italian for goodbye," he said, unlocking the car. "Are you trying to tell me something?"

"It's a traditional Gypsy drink. Tea, with fruit in it."

He ~~look~~ed doubtful. "Well, I'm willing to give it a try."

"Says the doomed man," Tonia added with a laugh. "Don't worry, you'll like it."

When they pulled onto her street, Tonia sat up with a glad cry, peering through the windshield.

"Hey, I didn't think you were that happy to get rid of me," Ben grumbled.

"Don't be so defensive. My aunt and uncle are here. Look."

A beat-up pickup truck attached to a small mobile home stood before Tonia's house.

Ben looked over to see a man and woman and two kids having a picnic on Tonia's lawn. When they stopped in front of the house, Tonia didn't wait for him to come around and open her door. She flung it wide herself and leaped out to hurry across the grass. He wrestled Godzilla from the back seat and followed more slowly.

She hugged them one by one, gathering them into a collective hug, then stood back with her hands clasping her uncle's.

He had dark curly hair, worn long, and a thick black mustache, both peppered with gray. His dark eyes twinkled at Tonia as he talked to her in a rapid string of Romani. Her aunt and girl cousin were dressed in long flowered skirts and loose blouses that might have looked odd a few years ago, but were very fashionable now. A long-legged boy of about seventeen stood by, watching and listening.

For all her pride in her heritage and her love of bright colors, gold and music, Tonia was an American woman. Ben had the feeling he was about to meet some real Gypsies. Though he hated himself for thinking it, he wondered if he should have left his wallet in the glove compartment.

Tonia looked back to see Ben following her slowly across the grass. She hurried to him, took his hand and pulled him forward. She was not surprised that her relatives immediately seemed to draw in on themselves. They eyed his odd burden, remaining cool but friendly as she introduced Uncle Stephan and Aunt Yana, Georgi and Alizia to him. She explained that they had just arrived from their home near Santa Barbara and planned to spend the summer traveling.

Tonia began to chatter about her new job as she unlocked the door and invited everyone inside the house. "This is my chance to learn more about the Rom for my book, *Kak* Stephan."

"That is good, if that is what you want to do. Gypsies won't read it. We are a people who talk—we tell stories to our children. Only *gajes* say we must learn to read."

"I know that, *Kak*," Tonia answered dryly. "My book will be for them, not so much for the Rom. I know you don't like to hear it," she added, "but I think it's wonderful that you've taken a job at that horse-breeding farm during the school year so Alizia and Georgi can finish high school."

"Ah, the Americans," Stephan said, gesturing impatiently. "They say the children must go to school."

"Would you rather have them be like some of the Gypsy children in Europe?" Tonia asked sharply, taking Godzilla from Ben and setting it in a corner of the living room. "Exploited by bosses who teach them to pick pockets and harass tourists. Some of them live in filth and have no one to care for them or teach them the Gypsy ways of *Wuzho*— ritual cleanliness," she explained for Ben's benefit.

Stephan's brows drew together in a vicious frown. "I spit on those who treat children thus."

Ben watched the older man regain control of his fierce expression.

After a moment, Stephan shrugged. "Anyway, we have no choice about sending Georgi and Alizia to school. Women with big boxes full of papers chase us down and ask many questions if our children do not go to school. They don't know that staying in one place too long brings bad luck. Gypsies must travel to stay in good luck."

"There are many things they don't understand about the Rom. That's why I'm going to write the book."

Tonia gestured everyone to seats, asked after her cousin's friends and perched on the arm of her aunt's chair.

"And where is Annie?" Yana asked, glancing around. "Traveling?"

Tonia exchanged a humored look with Ben who was beginning to understand that traveling, moving from place to place was the ultimate goal for this branch of the Meier family. "Yes. She went on a cruise."

Yana sat up straight and clutched at Tonia's hand. "You mean on water."

This time Tonia couldn't help laughing as she gave her aunt a reassuring pat. "That's the way cruises are usually taken."

"It is not good to leave the land. The earth is what one needs," Yana declared, shaking her head.

As they talked, Ben watched Tonia's indulgent interplay with her young cousins. Georgi seemed to have something of a crush on her. Although there was nothing pretentious about Tonia, to the young boy she must have seemed very sophisticated. Ben was touched to note how Tonia seemed to acknowledge Georgi's feelings without making him feel foolish. Alizia also seemed to look up to her older cousin.

As she talked, Tonia studied Ben's face, trying to decipher his enigmatic look and discover what he thought of her relatives.

He appeared intent on her explanations. Though their plans for the remainder of the day had been spoiled by the arrival of her relatives, he didn't seem to mind. He was watching her with her family as though he found them fascinating, but she wondered what conclusions he would draw, knowing his bent for snap judgments.

Tonia's sparkling chatter was an effort to put off the moment when her uncle would turn his attention to Ben. She could see Stephan sizing him up.

Stephan was even tempered and loving, but he was protective of his family and not unwilling to make a fast buck.

Before she could prevent whatever Stephan might be planning, her aunt gave her an injured look and said, "Antonia, your *mamio* would be very disappointed in you if you did not offer us something to drink."

Embarrassed at having to be reminded of her manners, she said, "I was going to make *chao* for Ben. He's never had our tea."

Although reluctant to leave Ben at the mercy of her freewheeling, opinionated uncle, she reminded herself that Ben's own uncle was the same way. He should be able to hold his own, she decided as she went into the kitchen.

When the door swung shut behind them, her aunt asked, "Where did you meet this *gaje*?"

"He's my employer's nephew. I've only known him a couple of weeks."

Yana tossed her long gray-streaked braid back over her shoulder and opened the refrigerator to find lemons and oranges. "And has he talked to your mother?"

"That would be impossible, since she's gone, *Bibi* Yana."

Tonia stepped outside to retrieve a jar of sun tea she had made and set outside early that morning. After warming in the sun all day, the tea was strong and fresh.

"So you don't have your mother's permission to be courted by this young man?" Yana persisted.

"*Bibi*," Tonia said, trying to be firm but kind. "I'm twenty-three. I don't follow the Gypsy ways in this. I will choose my own man. Ben and I hardly know each other.

Besides, what will you do if Alizia falls in love? You can't lock her up. In many ways she is like me—more American than Gypsy."

Yana swung around and placed her hands on her ample hips. She looked very offended by Tonia's observation. "We will deal with that when the time is right. My daughter will do as she is told. So," she continued, refusing to be deflected from her purpose, "you think you know better than your elders? You think you can arrange a better marriage than your mother could? What about that Gregory?" she asked, putting the accent on the second syllable in a roll of disgust, much as an Eastern European would.

Tonia threw up her hands. "Greg was a mistake that I won't repeat, but I'm not going to arrange anything or let *Mamio* arrange anything for me. When I marry, it will be for love."

Yana snorted. "Love! That comes later, after the babies. Tell me, do you love this *gaje*—this Ben?" She pronounced it "bean", making Tonia smile before frowning at the question.

Did she? Early this morning, after his outrageous statement that he had the "sick feeling" he could fall in love with her, she would have said an unequivocal no. Moments later, seeing his exhaustion and vulnerability, she might have answered in the affirmative. Now she wasn't so sure. There were a great many things about him to love but, as he had said, how well did they know each other?

"You have no answer? 'An unsure heart makes for unsteady hands,' as my mother would have said. When you don't know your mind, you know nothing."

"I don't see how those two statements go together. When I am ready for love and marriage, I will know."

"Hmph," Yana snorted, picking up a knife and slicing violently at the fruit. "With a *gaje*? That kind of marriage doesn't work. You should marry one of the Rom. When we do otherwise, the Gypsy ways will die out. Unless..." Yana's eyes gleamed. "Unless the *gaje* is willing to embrace Gypsy customs." She began dropping fruit slices into a glass pitcher that Tonia had taken from the cabinet. "I will speak to your uncle about it. In the absence of your father, it is his place to talk to the *gaje*."

Tonia nearly dropped the pitcher. "No, *Bibi* Yana," she begged. "Please don't. You are building this up in your mind when there is no reason to."

Tonia let the subject drop when the door swung open and Alizia came into the kitchen, but she could tell from the determined set of her aunt's chin that it wasn't ended. She heartily wished that her mother was home. Annie Meier had a way of reconciling the Gypsy ways with her own liberated American ideas that pacified her late husband's relatives. Tonia didn't have that gift and often ended up frustrated with them and herself.

She led the way back to the living room and stopped dead when she heard her uncle saying, "But our family knows nothing about you. As Antonia's only living male relative, I feel I must ask your intentions toward her. If her grandfather was still alive he would be talking to you. He was a good man." Stephan paused. "For a *gaje*."

"Uncle Stephan!"

The older man turned to look over his shoulder at her. "Antonia, I will take care of this."

"No!" She hurried forward, slapped the tea tray down on the coffee table and clamped her hands onto her hips. "Uncle Stephan, you're embarrassing me!"

"I am only thinking of you, my *shey*. I want to know what this young man has on his mind."

"Leaving, if he's got the good sense I think he's got."

Ben held his hand up. "It's all right, Tonia. I want to hear what your uncle has to say."

Tonia turned her stunned gaze on him, to see that, although his face was grave, his eyes held a humorous twinkle.

"But..."

"I think this is important to your Uncle Stephan."

Tonia looked at her aunt's determined face. The older woman nodded in approval.

Tonia knew Ben was right—acting the part of the family patriarch was important to Stephan. If she didn't allow it, he would lose face before his family, a hard blow for a man as proud as her uncle. She just wished she knew exactly what Ben was thinking. She hoped he wasn't secretly making fun of her family. Finding humor in their ways was one thing, mocking them was another. Still, he had a point about the importance of this to Stephan.

"All right," she said, sinking down onto the arm of the sofa.

With an officious nod, Stephan prepared to do business. He pulled at the cuffs of his white shirt, smoothed his salt and pepper mustache and assumed the same sorrowful expression he had worn the time she had seen him sell a deaf horse to an unsuspecting man. "Our Tonia has no father or grandfather to speak for her so I feel it is my duty."

"I understand," Ben said solemnly.

Tonia barely stopped herself from rolling her eyes at his concerned expression.

"The family has grave objections to her marrying a non-Gypsy. There are many Gypsy ways that must not die out," Stephan continued. Yana nodded in the background, tossing her niece an I-told-you-so look.

"I understand, sir."

"But sometimes we cannot talk to the young ones. They have their own ideas—ideas they get from the television and from schools. They think they must choose for themselves."

Ben sucked his bottom lip in and bit down on it as though commiserating with Stephan's dilemma. Tonia suspected he was trying not to laugh.

"So, Tonia can choose for herself," Stephan turned his rough hands palms up in a gesture of hopelessness. His big brown eyes looked ready to weep. "That is the way things are done now. But we cannot let her go without a proper *daro*."

Tonia nearly tumbled onto the floor. "Uncle Stephan!"

"Wait, wait now, little one," Stephan waved his hand like a pontiff calming an insurgent.

Ben cleared his throat. "I may regret asking this, but what is a *daro*, Stephan?"

"A bride price."

"Like a dowry?" Ben's eyebrows rose. "You mean you'll let me marry Tonia and you'll throw in a few goats or other livestock, too?"

The family gasped in shock, and Stephan gave him an injured look. "Of course not. You must pay *us* for the privilege of marrying our child."

CHAPTER SEVEN

TONIA PLANTED her elbow on the back of the sofa and dropped her forehead into her palm, wishing the floor would open up and swallow her. Ben seemed to be amused by the whole conversation. At least he couldn't be suspicious of Stephan's motives—his only one was greed.

Ben chewed his lip for a moment as if deep in thought. When he spoke, his voice had an odd squeak. "And what would you consider to be a fair, uh, *daro*?"

"Antonia has been to college."

"Yes, I know. Does that raise the price?"

"An educated Romani woman is very rare."

"Especially one like her," Ben agreed.

Tonia wanted to kick them both. They sounded like they were bargaining for a mare.

"She has also taken care of her grandfather, and she is respectful to her mother."

"Good teeth, too," Ben added, still chewing his lip.

Tonia bared her teeth at him. Ben caught the gesture and jerked his eyes away from her, coughing violently into his fist.

"Yes, I would say she is a good woman—would make a good wife, breed fine sons."

Tonia's spine stiffened. "I have no intention of breeding any...."

Seeing that his niece was out of patience, Stephan suddenly dropped his role as uncle-protector and seemed to make up his mind to conclude the negotiations. "Five thousand dollars," he announced.

"Five thousand." Ben's eyes widened. "Hmmm. That's a bit steep."

"She is worth it."

"Can she cook?"

"I can't even open a frozen dinner."

Stephan threw her a thunderous look. "Like a dream."

"Well, I think half that much would be more in line," Ben said.

Stephan puffed out his chest and summoned a look of outrage. "Two thousand five hundred dollars for such a fine woman?"

"She can be a bit sassy, you know."

Tonia jerked upright. "Sassy!"

"It's the American influence. The family can't be held responsible for that," Stephan disclaimed. "Four thousand."

Stephan was an old hand at bargaining but when Tonia saw his eyes shift slightly, she feared he was losing this deal. He didn't know Ben and couldn't be sure whether or not the younger man was really interested in marrying her.

"Three thousand," Ben countered.

"Done."

Both men sat back with satisfied smiles.

"One question, though, Stephan," Ben said. "Who gets the money? And when?"

Stephan tried to resume his concerned-uncle expression. "Well, it is given after the wedding. Since Tonia is very precious to our family, I think it would be fair if her mother and I shared it."

Tonia gave him a sardonic look. "Not if Mother has anything to say about it."

Watching her face, Ben chuckled. "We'll wait and discuss it when Mrs. Meier gets home. Now—" he rubbed his palms together "—tell me what I need to know about Gypsy weddings."

With a low sound of disgust, Tonia started to get up to leave the room. Ben slid off the sofa and grabbed her hand before she got more than a few inches away. He tumbled her down beside him and held her there.

While she fumed, Ben grasped her hand. As they sipped the *chao*, Yana described the traditional Gypsy wedding, which usually followed a civil or religious ceremony.

The young couple, she said, was given salted bread, which they broke and ate in the presence of their families and friends. The feasting lasted for three days and nights and the newly married couple weren't allowed to sleep together until the third night. This pronouncement brought a fierce scowl to Ben's face that sent Alizia into peals of laughter.

"Maybe we won't follow all the Gypsy wedding customs," he said.

Two hours later, Tonia stood alone at the door, waving goodbye to her relatives. Ben had followed her uncle outside where they talked earnestly, Ben with his head down and his hands in his pockets. They had shaken hands as Ben turned back to the house, whistling. He went inside while she told her family goodbye. They promised to stop by again on their way home in late summer.

Their next stop would be several days' stay with Yana's sister in Arizona. As they drove off, Tonia wondered how much longer Georgi and Alizia would be content to live the way their parents did. Their summer-long treks kept the kids away from their friends and normal routine. She knew that in spite of their parents' opposition, both Georgi and Alizia intended to go to college.

Tonia had quietly promised Georgi she would begin researching scholarships in an attempt to get him into the eastern technical college he longed to attend. She knew the sparks would fly when they told Stephan and Yana.

As she stood watching, the truck and trailer turned the corner and passed out of sight. She no longer had a reason to stay outside, but she hesitated to go back in.

She dreaded facing Ben, discovering what impression he had of her relatives. She was embarrassed by her uncle's machinations and irritated with Ben. Stephan had always been devious and would never change, she knew. But it hadn't been necessary for Ben to encourage her wily uncle.

Chilled, she hugged her arms around herself, went inside, and shut the door.

Ben was sprawled on the sofa with one arm along the back, the other propped behind his head. His long legs were stretched out before him. If he'd been in his own house, he probably would have rested them on the coffee table.

"You didn't have to go along with him," Tonia accused, moving into the room.

He turned his face toward her and blessed her with a lazy grin. His hand lifted to beckon her to him. "Along with whom?"

Tonia ignored the gesture. "Uncle Stephan. You two sounded like a couple of horse traders, and I was the prize mare."

"It seemed important to your uncle. And we should keep the family happy. Besides, isn't a *daro* traditional?" He patted the cushion beside him. When she still didn't move, he pulled his feet in and sat up straight, turning halfway around to face her.

"Well, yes."

"And tradition means a lot to your family."

He sounded so sensible, she was wary. "Yes."

Ben got up and sauntered over to her. "Especially since they were afraid of your marrying, a, uh, *gaje*. I suppose that was what your aunt was talking to you about in the kitchen?"

"How did you know?"

"You both looked very unhappy when you came out. Your Aunt Yana was obviously worried about you. I thought bargaining with your uncle would set their minds at rest." He took her chilly hands in his and chafed them for a moment. He placed a kiss in the center of her palms and settled them on each side of his face.

The touch of her sensitive palms on his skin jolted her, adding to her confusion.

"You don't have to worry about setting their minds at rest," she mumbled, trying to pull her hands away. Ben grasped her wrists, gave a tug, and she tumbled against him.

"But I do have to be concerned about what your family thinks. We don't want dissension about our marriage." Ben positioned her so that she was snuggled intimately against him. He moved his knees apart to capture one of hers between them.

His closeness made her tremble. "But we aren't married."

Ben bent his head. "Not yet."

Something was choking off her breath. Was it her heart that had jumped into her throat as his lips started closing in on hers? "We aren't *getting* married."

Something dark and exciting moved in his eyes. "You wanna make a bet?"

Ben loosened the hold he had on her wrists, but she was too surprised to move them. Her hands stayed suspended in midair as he slid one arm around her waist. His other hand cupped the side of her face, tilting her head until it was lying against his shoulder. Off balance she could do nothing but slide her hands around his shoulders and cling.

Ben's lips seemed to take a long time to reach hers. Tension twisted in her so that when their mouths finally touched, she felt something akin to an electric shock.

Startled, she drew away. "Wh-what did you say?"

"We're getting married." He nuzzled her ear.

What he was doing and saying swamped her senses. She couldn't let this happen. "Like heck we are!" she gasped.

She tried to pull out of his arms, and Ben let her go.

"Tonia, I don't think your uncle, or mine, would go along with our just living together. Your uncle would take a horsewhip to me, and Hank would skin me with his antique Bowie knife. So, shall we set the date?"

Tonia held a hand to her forehead.

"Wait. Wait a minute." She took a deep breath and steadied herself. For once she wasn't going to listen to his glib tongue and be carried away by his persuasiveness.

"The date's negotiable. How about in two months? That should give us plenty of time to make wedding plans."

"No, Ben—"

"Next month, then."

"Stop!"

"Next week?"

"Ben, don't...."

"Tomorrow, and that's my final offer." He pretended to mop his brow. "You drive an even harder bargain than Stephan does."

Tonia reached out and grabbed his arm, giving him a hard shake. "Ben, we're not getting married!"

He went very still. "Why not?"

"We've only known each other a few weeks!"

Ben dismissed that with a wave. He rubbed his hands together and started pacing the room in excitement. "Long

enough. Do you think Hank will be pleased?" He stopped
to consider that for a moment. "I don't really care. *I'm*
pleased. When is your mother due back? We can wait till
then, if it isn't too long. Maybe you could call her."

"Ben!"

Tonia's frantic shout finally jerked him around to face
her. She was pale. Her eyes were huge and dark.

He grimaced and crossed to take her into his arms again.
"I'm sorry, honey. I'm going too fast for you. It's just that
now that I've made up my mind, I can't wait to get arrangements made."

"Why?"

"Well, it seems silly to waste—"

Her ponytail whipped from side to side as she shook her
head. "I mean why do you want to marry me?"

"Because it just occurred to me that you're exactly what
I've been looking for—although I didn't know I was looking. You're independent and determined, but you care about
your family—and my eccentric uncle. You accept people the
way they are, let them be themselves. I think you would be
that way with me." He pushed a strand of hair from her face
and hooked it behind her ear. "We would be good for each
other, wouldn't we?"

Tonia was so dizzy she laid her head against his chest. She
could hear the steady beat of his heart while her own was
pounding. "I don't know, Ben. You said this morning that
you were scared, didn't know if you loved me."

His cheek rested against her hair. From the movement of
his facial muscles, she knew he was smiling. "I have the
feeling that will take care of itself. How about it? Let's get
married."

"This is happening too fast. You weren't sure of your
feelings, now you want to get married. People don't make
up their minds that fast."

"I do."

Yes, he did. What she had seen in his palm told her he took a long time to reach a decision, but once made, he acted on it instantly.

But she didn't.

"Will you at least think about it, Tonia?"

"Yes," she said into the front of his shirt.

"While you are, think about this," he said, tipping her head back for another kiss.

As his mouth moved over hers, Tonia knew she would be better off doing her thinking without him around, but she didn't protest when he maneuvered her toward the couch.

"This isn't fair," she whimpered.

"Nope."

"You're taking advantage of me, confusing me."

"Yup."

"Aren't you ashamed of yourself?"

"Nope."

"You're shameless."

"Yup. Why don't you stop talking now and kiss me back?"

With a throaty laugh, she did.

"Touch me, Tonia."

She sighed his name and slid her hands hesitantly over his shoulders.

"Touch me," he said again, reaching up to press her hands to him. He settled them at his waist and lifted his sweater so that she was touching his skin. She quivered, but her untutored hands didn't move further.

"Ben," she whispered in her embarrassment. "I don't know how to touch you."

"Of course you do, darling," he said, kissing her again.

"No, I don't." She was afraid he would think she was being coy.

Ben's hands stopped their roaming exploration of her back. He drew away and looked down at her. The passionate glaze in his eyes cleared. "Tonia, do you mean you've never...?"

She turned her face away. "Never. It is forbidden."

"Forbidden? By who?"

"By Gypsy tradition. A woman who isn't a virgin at her marriage is considered *marhime*, unclean."

"Antonia." He said her name in a tone that said he knew that wasn't the whole story.

Keeping her face turned, she spoke in a low voice. "Greg was the only guy I was ever serious about, and I guess I wasn't *that* serious."

"Thank God."

The relief in his voice had her turning to study him. "You mean you don't mind?"

"I'm glad. The thought of you and that jerk was driving me crazy." He hugged her, and his rueful laugh bounced her against his chest. "But what a wedding night we're going to have!"

Ben slid her off his lap and kissed her blushing face. "I'd better go. I'll call you in the morning."

She walked him to the door and watched him lope down the sidewalk. He turned when he reached the Jensen and waved to her. When he was gone, she stood with her back to the door, her fingers massaging her forehead.

This had happened too fast. Ben seemed so sure of himself while she was reeling from shock.

She had told Yana she would marry for love yet, despite his proposal, Ben hadn't said he loved her. Was Yana right, that love came later—heaven forbid—after the babies?

She needed to talk to someone. In her room, she flopped down on the bed and grabbed the phone. She had punched out three digits of Maria's phone number before she changed her mind, hung up, then plucked the receiver up again to call her mother.

"Tonia, darling," Annie said after Tonia's hello. "Is something wrong?"

"Well, not wrong, exactly."

"Are you ill? Is everything all right at work? Is Hank all right?"

"Yes, yes," Tonia hastened to reassure her. "It's nothing like that." She paused and decided to plunge right in. "Ben asked me to marry him."

There was a stunned silence on the other end of the line. "Why, Tonia, that's won—uh, Ben who?"

Tonia shook her head in consternation. No wonder her mother was floundering. She didn't know anything about Ben Andrews. Tonia had barely mentioned him. "You remember—Hank Tyson's nephew. We've seen each other several times."

Several? Tonia frowned. She could count the number on the fingers of one hand.

"And . . ." her mother prompted.

Tonia told her about their first meeting and what had happened since. She skipped over the aftermath of their visit to Old Town. Now was not the time to tell Annie about the house break-in. Before she could get to that day's events, Annie interrupted. "So you don't think he's sincere?"

"That's just it," Tonia sighed. "I *think* he is. He distrusted my interest in Hank, but he seems to have resolved that. I'm the one with doubts now. I'm afraid he just wants me. . . ."

"You mean physically? Love can grow from that."

"Now you sound like Aunt Yana."

"Yana? How did she get into it?"

Once again, Tonia found herself making a complicated explanation. Before she finished, Annie was laughing.

"You mean they bargained for you?"

"Yes," Tonia answered miserably.

"That's a good sign, my *shey*. This Benjamin Andrews must be serious about you if he's willing to go through that!"

Tonia sat up straight. Of course, she had known that. She had just needed someone else to say it. "I guess you're right."

"Of course I am," Annie stated. "I'm your mother."

"There's really nothing to worry about," Tonia went on. "He doesn't expect an answer right away. I'll have time to sort out my feelings."

"I know you'll make the right decision."

"If I say yes, you might be three thousand dollars richer," she said wryly. "Or fifteen hundred if Uncle Stephan has anything to say about it."

"We'll see about that!" Annie huffed, exactly as Tonia had known she would.

When they finished their mother-daughter talk, Tonia hung up and fell across her bed, smiling at the ceiling. She *would* make the right decision.

In Cabo San Lucas, Mexico, Annie Meier clasped her hands to the top of her head and spun in a joyous circle.

THE PHONE RANG early the next morning, and Tonia rolled over groaning. She had lain awake for hours with her mind forming and discarding plans about her relationship with Ben.

She tried to force her eyes open. Why did people call so early on the weekend? Didn't they know she liked to sleep in? It couldn't be her mother—they had just talked last night.

She started to bury her head under the pillow to wait the caller out, when she thought about Ben. He had said he would call. She sat up with a jerk and reached for the receiver.

"Tonia?" a woman's voice quavered over the line.

In the last mists of sleep she thought it was her mother, but the frantic tone alerted her. She came awake instantly, recognizing the voice. "Yes. Lucy?"

"Tonia, someone broke into Hank's house! I didn't know who else to call. His beautiful things. . . ."

Shuddering with a sense of déjà vu, Tonia gripped the phone. "Are you still in the house?"

"Yes, but—"

"Get out immediately. They may still be there."

"No, no. The police are here. They said someone in charge should come. Can you?"

Tonia was already up, grabbing her underthings from a drawer while she juggled the phone. "I'll be right there, Lucy. Don't panic. Do you have Ben's number? I don't." She almost burst into hysterical laughter. He had asked her to marry him, and she didn't even know his home phone number or exactly where he lived.

"You mean Hank's nephew? Yes, it's here on the desk."

"Call him right away. I'm on my way."

She hung up as a tearful Lucy said goodbye. Jerking on her clothes and grabbing a jacket, she was out the door in less than fifteen minutes. As she drove, vivid pictures of her ransacked home whirled in her mind. She tried not to imagine what Hank's vandalized home must look like, his valuables broken and scattered.

Two police cars stood at the curb before Hank's house. Ben pulled up behind her, and they dashed up the walk together.

A khaki-uniformed policeman introduced himself as Officer Marriott and pointed out Detective Rios of the robbery detail. Ben and Tonia were led inside where they stumbled to a halt in the living room doorway.

Tonia's house had only been ransacked. Hank's had been stripped!

The wall opposite the couch looked obscenely bare without the O'Keeffe painting spilling its bright poppies. All the other paintings were also missing. Hank's entire collection of antique knives and guns was gone. A faint film of dust outlined where each piece had lain.

"Oh, dear God," Ben breathed.

Tonia's shocked gaze followed his to the bare pedestal where Hank's Remington bronze horse had stood.

"We've got to find who did this before Hank gets home," Ben said in a dazed voice. "That horse was his favorite piece. Losing it will kill him."

Tonia groped for his hand and squeezed it.

"Mr. Andrews," Detective Rios spoke to the two shell-shocked people clutching each other in the living room door. "We need you to determine exactly what was taken. I understand the entire collection belongs to the home's owner, Henry Tyson, and that he's out of town."

The policeman's businesslike tone brought Ben out of his dazed state. He and Tonia set to work inventorying what had been taken. Besides most of Hank's art collection and Western artifacts, many of his rare books were gone.

"They must have had a good idea what they wanted," Marriott observed in disgust sometime later. "You'd think they had a shopping list."

Ben and Tonia exchanged glances. "I think they did," Ben said, and explained about the missing bibliography.

"The alarm system is off during the day because there are always so many people in and out of the house," Tonia said.

"Someone could have entered after watching Mr. Tyson and Miss Heller leave that morning," Officer Marriott speculated. "Whoever it was could have closed you two in the vault and taken the list. You say it was sitting out?"

"On top of the desk," Tonia said faintly. She had been going through the desk drawers to determine what was missing. Now she sat down abruptly in the chair, sickened that someone would purposely shut them in the vault.

The detective nodded and made some quick notes to himself on a small pad he carried. "They were damned smart in more ways than that," he observed.

"What do you mean?" Ben asked, standing up from his place before the bookcase and dusting off his slacks.

"They circumvented the alarm system last night. No small feat, since it was very sophisticated. State of the art. Besides the front door key, there was one to the alarm system."

"Yes," Ben said. "A thick plastic one with a magnetic strip like an automated-teller bank card."

"The burglars had both. Either they spent a long time planning this, or they had an accomplice inside the house. Maybe both."

Tonia sent a shocked look at Ben, who glanced at her, then away. She would have given anything to know what he was thinking—whether or not he suspected her. She turned back to the officer who didn't meet her eyes.

"I'd like to know who has both keys to the house," Rios concluded.

The den door opened and Lucy stepped in with a coffee tray. Her eyes were red-rimmed from crying, and her hands shook as she set the tray down on the desk.

"I have keys," Ben answered the policeman. "So does Hank, Miss Heller and Miss Meier."

"That's right."

"Are yours still in your possession?"

They both produced their keys. Ben from his pocket and Tonia from a zippered compartment of her purse.

"Miss Heller?"

The coffee carafe wobbled above the cup Lucy was holding. She barely kept from pouring the scalding brew over her hand. Carefully, she set both items down and looked up. Her pale topaz eyes, glittering with tears, went to the gaps in the bookcases then back to the officer. "Yes, sir?"

"Where are your keys now? Obviously you had them this morning."

"They're in my purse."

"You haven't lost them and had to get replacements?"

Tonia watched the officer's keen eyes go to the girl's shaking hands, as Lucy made a visible effort to control them.

"I misplaced them early last week, but I found them right where I thought they were." Her eyes darted from Tonia, to Ben, then to the policeman. "You know how it is when you change purses . . . well, I guess you don't know," she said, with a nod toward the men. "But things get misplaced."

Tonia took pity on the girl. "Yes, we know how it is. Thank you for making the coffee. Why don't you serve it? I could certainly use some."

Lucy nodded, calming a little.

"You think there was an accomplice in the house? You mean someone who had entered earlier?" Ben asked, going back to the officer's previous statement.

"No, I mean someone very familiar with the house." He hesitated. "An employee, I'm afraid, or a frequent visitor."

"That's impossible."

"I don't believe it."

Ben and Tonia spoke at the same moment.

"Maybe," the policeman answered. "But when we're dealing with articles this valuable, we have to consider everything."

He turned to Lucy. "Miss Heller. I'd like to ask you a few more questions."

Lucy set her cup down on the edge of the table. It tilted, and she righted it with a jerk, then looked up apologetically, her face red. "All right."

Tonia felt for the unnerved girl. Perhaps Lucy could handle this better without an audience. She stood up and motioned for Ben to follow her.

He gave her a distracted look and rose. "Let's go into the kitchen, Tonia. I'll see if I can contact Hank. The charter service he usually rents a boat from may be able to locate him."

They tracked Hank down by shortwave. He was deep-sea fishing off the coast of Mexico and promised to be home on the first available flight. He sounded so shaken, Ben was reluctant to tell him the full extent of his loss. Finally, he admitted that almost everything, including the Remington bronze, was gone.

Tonia listened with her fingers pressed to her lips, feeling Hank's pain.

When he hung up, Ben gripped the edge of the counter until his knuckles turned white. With his head low and his eyes focused on some point outside the window, he launched into a steady stream of cursing that frightened Tonia with its intensity.

"His collections are all he's had since Maggie died," Ben said savagely. "Whoever did this will pay," he vowed, his gray eyes cold as a Northern ice floe. "They'll pay."

"I haven't known Hank very long," she ventured, trying to help him deal with his intense feelings, "but I don't think that his collections were his whole life. Look at all the new friends he's made and...."

Ben turned his frosty gaze on her. "That's right. You haven't known him very long, Tonia. This business of writing a book, making new friends, taking off fishing every couple of weeks, is a phase he's going through. He's spent years and thousands of dollars on his art—and you think they're not important to him?"

"I didn't say that!"

He didn't seem to hear her. "Besides, someone—one of his new so-called friends—has taken advantage of him, accepted his hospitality, his help, then robbed him." His eyes glittered, going to where Lucy's jacket lay on a kitchen chair. "And I'm going to find out who." Ben turned away, cutting off anything she might have said. "Let's see if Rios needs us anymore. If not, I'll see you home. You can leave the other car here. I'll have someone deliver it to you later. Then I've got things to do."

Frustrated, Tonia stared after him, wondering if he seriously suspected Lucy. She couldn't ask because he had closed himself off from her, and she didn't know how to reach him.

Detective Rios asked them to get the second copy of Hank's bibliography out and check off exactly what was missing. That task finished, they left for Tonia's house by midafternoon.

Neither of them had eaten all day, so Tonia offered to fix sandwiches. Ben nodded and began pacing around her living room.

Disturbed, Tonia watched him for a moment. He was like a caged animal. She could feel his fury at the intruders who had violated his uncle's home and stolen from him. She also knew his frustration at his powerlessness.

He touched several items on the mantel, letting his hand close around a brass candlestick. She thought for a moment that he would throw it across the room in rage, but before she could call out a protest, he released it. Several of her animal miniatures were set at a new angle by his restless fingers.

He looked around, spotting the jacket Tonia had thrown down on the back of the sofa. Ben picked it up and started for the front closet where he knew she kept it.

Tonia realized he just needed something to occupy his hands. Through her mind flashed a vision of the messy closet she hadn't had time to clean since her break-in.

"Careful, don't open that, Ben," she said, half laughing in hopes of lightening the atmosphere. "You'll get the surprise of your life."

Ben gave her a curious look as his hand turned the knob.

Tonia grimaced. "Ben, don't—"

He swung the door open, snapped on the light and froze.

On top of the mess was perched a stack of books. It had been shrink-wrapped in plastic, but through it could be clearly read the titles on several of the volumes.

They all pertained to the Old West.

He picked up the heavy stack and turned it so the top volume faced him. The name engraved on the bottom right corner of the front cover was Henry E. Tyson.

CHAPTER EIGHT

BEN LIFTED the bound stack and straightened. "Is *this* why you didn't want me to open the closet, Tonia? Because these were hidden here?"

His voice was curiously flat, and when he turned to her, Tonia read the accusation in his eyes.

Since the day before, she had been grasping an illusion. Whatever his reasons for wanting marriage, love and trust weren't among them.

"Ben," she said in a level voice. "You had better think things over before you say anything you'll regret."

"I am thinking," he said. "I'm thinking that a lot of little things are adding up. Getting a job with Hank was very easy and convenient for you. The night your home was broken into you were very anxious that I stay. Was that so I could tell the police later that everything was fine when we left? So these things could be dropped off here later?"

Tonia gasped. "Why would I have that done to my own house!"

"I'm not sure, but nothing was stolen and—" he waved his hand toward her bookcase of tiny animals "—nothing was broken."

"Of all the crazy..."

Ignoring her, Ben went on relentlessly. "Yesterday you said you would give anything to own a rare book like that volume of Dickens we saw at the library. Today you said Hank's collection wasn't that important to him anymore.

Now I find part of it in your closet. Where's the rest, and who else was in on it? You'd better explain."

A cold stubborn fury settled over her features. "All right! If I had wanted to hide those books, would I have put them in plain sight in the closet?"

"I don't know, why don't *you* tell *me*?"

"The fact is, those books weren't hidden. Nor are they stolen. Those are some books Hank had me take to the bindery last week. I picked them up for him. When we went to Old Town you sought *me* out. You wanted us both to go in your car." Tonia reached up and rapped her knuckles against her forehead. "Fool that I am, I wanted you to stay that night."

Uncertainty flickered in his eyes. "Tonia..."

"Let me finish," she insisted, stabbing a finger at his chest. "I have the right to defend myself. At the library I wasn't even looking at the Dickens when I said what I did. I was thinking about the history of Europe that was right next to it. It probably has information about Gypsies." She paused, breathing hard, planning her next furious defense.

Ben stared at her for a moment, then lifted the books to his hips, cradling them under his arm. He shut the closet door and kept his eyes fixed on it for a moment. A deep sigh gusted through his clenched teeth. "Maybe I shouldn't have said that," he said.

"No, Ben. You shouldn't have *thought* it."

"Look, Tonia. I'm sorry...."

"Are you?" she asked, studying his face. Her dark eyes mirrored the hurt and misery she felt. "Maybe we shouldn't talk about this now. We're both tired and upset."

"Let me explain."

"Do you know what you said?" she burst out, clutching her arms across her waist. She blinked back tears as she faced him. "Yesterday you said you had the sick feeling I was the kind of girl you could fall in love with. Ben, you always came to *me*. You took me to Old Town for dinner. When my house was vandalized, you comforted me—ignored me for a week, then showed up to take me out again. I went because I thought I was falling in love with you, and I thought you felt the same."

By the time she finished, she could no longer blink back the tears. They began running down her cheeks. Ben started to speak, but she held up shaking hands to stop him. "No—" she gasped. "You bargained with my uncle for me. I thought you were serious. *He* thought you were serious. You gave me that fine speech about pleasing our families. It must have been some kind of joke."

"No. I didn't treat it as a joke." The harshness in Ben's voice echoed his growing anger.

"Then what was it to you? You couldn't have meant it."

"You're blowing this out of proportion," he said impatiently. "Consider the circumstances."

The heels of her hands swiped at her wet face. "That's just it. The real problem comes back to trust. You don't trust me. You never have. I don't think you're capable of it." She held up both hands when he started to protest. "All right, I understand that you were hurt by someone, and that you're afraid of looking foolish over a woman, but what is the time limit on that? Does every woman you meet have to pay for it?"

Ben's face was flushed, his lips pulled into a thin line that stretched the skin downward. His hands shot out to grasp her shoulders, forcing her to look at him. "Dammit, Tonia. Listen to me. I meant it when I bargained with your uncle for you. I followed him outside to be sure he understood I had every intention of marrying you."

"Why?" she asked on an incredulous laugh. "When you think I would steal from my employer?" She paused, her eyes widening and her mouth forming an astonished O. "Do you think it runs in the family? Would you think that if I wasn't a Gypsy?"

"I shouldn't have thought it—I don't think it," Ben said, turning suddenly to stride over and pick up his coat. He set the stack of books down and jammed his arms into the sleeves. "But you won't listen. Maybe I didn't have a good reason for being distrustful. You have *no* reason for your overgrown pride. You've got a chip on your shoulder about your heritage, did you know that?"

Tonia glared at him. She refused to justify that ridiculous statement with an argument. He was in the wrong, not her. "I think you'd better go. I don't think I want to see you again."

The look he gave her should have singed her eyebrows off.

He settled his jacket over his shoulders with a jerk. "I'm going. If you feel like accepting my apology, you know where to reach me."

Palms up, Tonia's hands flew wide in helpless disbelief. "That shows how much you know. I don't have your number—the man I was considering marrying—and I don't even know where you live!"

He reached into his pocket and took out his wallet. From a small case inside he pulled a business card. With a few bold slashes of a pen he scribbled his home phone number on it and held it out to her. When she didn't accept it immediately, he grabbed her hand and slapped it into her palm. Retaining hold of her wrist, he pulled her toward him.

Thinking he would try to kiss her, Tonia turned her head away. Instead, he nudged her hair aside with his nose and whispered. "See you, Tonia. Call me."

With that, he jerked the door open and stalked out.

Tonia slammed it behind him and whirled away. He was acting as if *she* was the one in the wrong.

Her agitated pacing carried her to the window where she stared out at the lengthening shadows across the patio. She leaned her head against the glass, deep in thought.

Ben could be just as much a suspect as she was, Tonia realized. He had keys to Hank's house. He knew the value of Hank's collection, probably to the penny. Granted, he had been inside the vault with her when the door shut. It was possible that he had fixed the door to shut somehow, or distracted her so an accomplice could.

That was possible. It had been the first time she had ever seen the teasing, humorous side of him. That alone had been enough to disarm her.

Why would he? her conscience asked.

He had expensive tastes, she concluded, thinking of his cars.

That wasn't enough reason to turn to theft.

Unless—

She straightened. Unless his business was in trouble. She recalled the night they'd had dinner in Old Town. Ben had left the table for a call from his secretary and returned to say his plans for expansion into Arizona and New Mexico would have to be put on hold. Later the next week he'd made a business trip to Arizona to try to save the deal.

Into her mind flashed a picture of Ben from the first time she had ever seen him. Standing on the beach talking to her, the thing uppermost in his mind had been his uncle. Hank's strange behavior, his change from a depressed old man into a prank-playing kid—all the changes and the new people in his life had worried Ben.

Ben's concern hadn't been faked. He loved his uncle and would never hurt him.

Tonia moved across to a chair.

No, he wouldn't steal from Hank, but he had thought that *she* would.

She was very, very glad she hadn't made love with Ben. If she had, not only would she now be feeling betrayed, but also *marhime*, unclean.

The sharp ring of the telephone jerked her out of her thoughts. She hurried into the kitchen and stared at it through two more rings, afraid it might be Ben. Finally, she snatched it up.

For the second time that day, Lucy Heller's soft voice quavered over the line. "Hello... Tonia?"

Despite her own misery, Tonia felt a surge of pity for the younger girl. She always started conversations as if afraid of rejection. Though she didn't feel up to it, she tried to infuse warmth into her voice. "Hello, Lucy. Are you at your apartment? Did the police leave Hank's house?"

"Yes." Lucy barely spoke above a whisper, and Tonia had to strain to hear her. "They finished up at the house right after you left. Mr. Andrews called to say he would be over to stay in the house until Hank gets back, so when he arrived I came home."

"Oh, well...good. Try to rest tonight. Hank will need us when he gets home."

"I know. Oh, Tonia—" Her voice broke. "All his beautiful things—gone. He spent so much time and money on them. I used to think that rich people who collected things were just showing off, but Hank's not like that. He's such a nice man."

She paused, and Tonia could feel the girl's distress over what had happened. Before she could reply, Lucy went on, "I was just wondering, do you—do you think the thieves will be caught?"

"Absolutely! When they do they'll go to jail, too—don't you worry. Ben will make sure the thieves are locked up for a long time." Tonia shuddered, remembering the fury on Ben's face.

There was a long silence on the other end of the phone. For a moment, Tonia thought Lucy had hung up. Finally Lucy said, "Do you think the officer really believed there was an—an accomplice in the house?"

"I'm afraid they'll suspect all of us, Lucy, until this is cleared up. Everyone who's been in the house."

"Oh," came the faint reply. "I wanted to know..."

"Yes, Lucy?" Tonia was becoming alarmed at the girl's frightened tone.

"I—oh, dear, I can't talk now. My brother just came in. I've got to go."

She hung up quickly, leaving Tonia staring at the receiver in her hand. What was that all about? She replaced the receiver wondering if Lucy would call back to confide in her.

SHE WAS DREAMING. She knew it, but she wasn't scared.

The beach opened up before her, and she recognized it as the section behind Hank's house. There were no sunbathers or joggers out, no children making sand castles or carrying boogie-boards into the surf.

With the dreamer's certainty, she knew she had gone for a walk along the beach. Turning back toward Hank's house, she saw a stream of dark figures, like ants, coming from his home. Each one carried a painting or one of his other treasures.

Tonia started to run, shouting for them to stop. They didn't turn around, but continued in lockstep away from the house. She ran harder, her face contorted with anger and concentration, her chest burning from the unusual effort. A cramp stitched itself into her side. Her speed was hampered by the sand that shifted under her feet.

With agonizing slowness, she gained on them, shouting and waving her arms.

Without stopping, the line of figures turned their heads toward her.

They all had Ben's face.

She screamed and didn't stop. The sound went on and on, long after her breath would have run out. Tonia stirred groggily and realized it wasn't a dream, but her burglar alarm.

Heart pounding, she sat up and threw off the covers. If she hadn't been so disoriented from her restless night and disturbingly real dream, she would have called the emergency number for the police. Instead, she stumbled toward the electronic box in the front hall that held the controls. Her fumbling fingers jerked the handle to shut off the noise.

She breathed a sigh of relief at the sudden quiet. It was followed almost immediately by a fierce pounding on the front door.

"Tonia! Antonia Marie Meier, let me in! Are you all right?"

"Mamio?" she gasped.

In a few moments, she had the door unlocked, and she and her mother were falling into each other's arms.

Elegant in a suit she had designed herself, with her dark hair pulled back into a neat chignon, Annie Meier looked so normal that tears stung Tonia's eyes.

Annie took one look at her distraught and disheveled child and hustled her back inside.

"What is going on here? What was that awful noise? My key won't work anymore! I tried jiggling the handle, thinking it was stuck, and that shrieking started!" Her questions and exclamations tumbled out as she pushed Tonia toward the couch. They sat down together, and Annie began rubbing Tonia's cold hands between her own.

In broken sentences, Tonia explained about the burglar alarm.

"Why do we need that?"

Because she had told her mother nothing about the break-in, Tonia guiltily glossed over a description of what had happened. "Nothing was taken," she hastened to add.

"I had a right to know," Annie pointed out. "It's my home, too."

"I didn't want to worry you. I didn't think it would happen again since Hank bought me all these alarms and locks and things. Not that they did much good on his house." She clasped her mother's hand once again for comfort. "*Mamio*, his house was broken into on Friday night or early Saturday morning. All of his collections were stolen. His art—everything. Ben thinks the shock might kill him."

Annie shook her head firmly. "Now, now, dear. That won't happen. He isn't that kind of man."

"How do you know?"

Annie looked startled. "Oh, I just meant—if he was going to die from a loss, he would have done so after losing his wife, wouldn't he? Didn't you say he was devoted to her?"

"Yes."

"Stop worrying," her mother commanded. "He'll come through this. And his things might be recovered. Anyway, all that doesn't explain why you didn't tell me that someone had broken into *our* house."

"No, I guess not," Tonia admitted, shamefaced. "But Hank convinced me not to."

Annie stood up and placed her hands on her hips. "Oh, he did, did he? That's why he was going to buy you a dog, isn't it? Well, I think I'm going to have to have a talk with that man."

Her brow furrowed, but then she seemed to remember that frowning causes wrinkles, and she smoothed her expression. Tonia smiled at the characteristic gesture.

Annie looked tanned and rested after her cruise and long vacation in Mexico. In fact, Tonia noted, she had gained a few pounds and the plumpness was pleasing. Her midnight black eyes had their old sparkle, and there was a glow about her face that wasn't dimmed by the intense look she was giving her daughter.

"*Mamio*, you look good."

Annie grinned at her. "Isn't that part of what Red Skelton says are the three ages of man? Young, middle-aged, and 'Gee, you look good'? Now," she said briskly, "why don't you get dressed while I bring in my bags? If we have time, we'll have some breakfast then go over to that man's house. Do you think he will be home yet?"

Lost in thought, it took Tonia a moment to understand that Annie wanted to go over to Hank's.

"I suppose so. He was expected back early this morning—but I can't go," she gasped.

"And why not?"

"Ben will be there."

Tonia explained what had happened between Ben and herself. "I thought that, even though we had doubts, we could work things out in time, but it's turned into a nightmare," she concluded, thinking of the dream she had just had.

"Hmph," her mother snorted. "It sounds like you let your heart rule your head. Did you think that because he had proposed to you he couldn't suspect you of theft?"

"Well, of course!"

"You were foolish, then."

"Me!"

"You probably became hurt and defensive right away, didn't you?"

"Well...."

"I knew it." Annie sat down again and slipped her arm around Tonia's shoulders. "It is possible to love and still suspect the loved one of wrongdoing. Wise love doesn't blind one to the other's faults, it accepts them."

"Ben doesn't love me."

"He does. He just doesn't know it. Do you love him?"

"Yes," Tonia sighed.

"Then you must accept the way he makes snap judgments."

Tonia knew her mother was right. The streak of flat Gypsy practicality that she had only traces of ran deep in her mother. "But I still feel so hurt by what he said, *Mamio*. How is it that this misunderstanding has turned out to be my fault?"

Annie laughed and hugged her. "Sometimes the one least at fault must be the one to forgive first. It has to start somewhere. Now, get dressed. We must go."

Tonia pulled on a robe and helped bring in suitcases from where the taxi driver had left them at the curb.

Annie darted around the house, exclaiming over changes that Tonia had made, checking on her plants, and asking after friends and family.

As she dressed, Tonia talked of Stephan and Yana's visit. Even hearing the story for the second time made Annie laugh until tears filled her eyes.

She was sitting on the side of the tub, watching Tonia put on her makeup.

"That Stephan! I've often told Yana, if I had seen him first, I probably would have married him instead of your father."

Tonia pulled a hairbrush through her hair and smiled to herself in the mirror. "It wouldn't have worked. You're too tall for him."

A troubled look passed over Annie's face.

"What's wrong?"

"My *shey*, would you mind if I did marry again? Sometime in the future," she hastened to add.

"Mind! I would be thrilled." Her brush clattered to the sink. "Have you met someone?"

Annie's flawlessly polished nails picked at an imaginary piece of lint on her skirt. "I can't talk about it yet—so don't you go jumping to conclusions."

Tonia's mind reeled. She could never remember her mother even dating regularly, much less considering marriage.

Annie stood up. "You look lovely, darling," she said, admiring the flaming red shirt and slacks her daughter had put on. "Now let's go. Hank Tyson probably needs our help."

"Can't I even have breakfast?"

"And don't whine. It's very unbecoming."

With a sigh of amused exasperation, Tonia led her mother out to Hank's car, which had been delivered while Tonia had been sleeping. Annie exclaimed over it. She had sold her own car just before leaving, planning to buy a new one when she returned. Hank's car, she said, was exactly what she liked.

"Hank just bought this," Tonia explained, watching her mother's face flush a strange shade of pink.

"He did? Oh, what a sweet thing to do—I mean, to let you drive his new car."

"Uh, yeah."

The morning's events had happened so quickly, Tonia didn't think to ask why Annie was accompanying her until they were almost to Del Mar. To her amazement, her mother blushed again.

"You said you wanted me to meet your boss someday," she said. "Oh, look, they've finished that new entrance to the racetrack. It looks much better than the old one."

Tonia gave her a puzzled look, wanting to ask why her mother was behaving so strangely, but moments later they were pulling onto Hank's street, and she was jolted by the sight of Ben's Jensen in the driveway. She had known he would be there, but she wasn't prepared to face him.

Lucy let them in, greeting Annie with downcast eyes still red-rimmed from crying. She offered to make coffee, and Tonia agreed. It seemed vital to Lucy to keep busy, although she had made enough coffee the previous day to float a good-sized battleship.

Tonia wanted to ask Lucy the reason for her call the night before, but Hank came through the living room doorway, distracting her. His normally animated face was deeply lined with worry, and his blue eyes had lost their devilish sparkle.

Ben was right behind him, his eyes searching her out. A look passed between them. His gaze was full of questions and regrets and apologies. Her eyes mirrored his.

She turned to introduce her mother to the two men—only to discover there was no need.

Annie walked toward Hank with her hands outstretched, and he took her in his arms and gave her a kiss full on the mouth.

"Hello, honey. I guess you heard about the robbery," he said. "Thanks for coming over. I need you with me now. You got home from the airport okay? I should have picked you up myself."

"It's all right, darling," Annie replied, putting her arms around him. "I knew you wanted to get home. This has all happened so fast. I wish we hadn't had to leave behind that huge tuna we caught."

It took Tonia several seconds to realize that her mother was kissing a man she supposedly had never met before!

"Mother!" she gasped.

"Hank!" Ben thundered.

Tonia glanced at Ben to see his face drawn into a perfect caricature of surprise. His mouth hung slack and his eyes bulged. If she hadn't been suffering shock herself, she would have laughed.

Their loud exclamations had the older couple turning around to face them.

Smiling graciously, Annie walked over and held her hand out to Ben. "Hello, Ben. I'm so glad to meet you at last. Hank and Tonia have told me so much about you."

Like an automaton, he lifted a limp hand to shake hers. He opened his mouth, closed it, gulped and finally asked, "When?"

"I beg your pardon?"

"When did Hank tell you all about me?"

"Let's go sit down, and we'll talk about it," Hank said in a voice devoid of its usual briskness. "I guess we've got some explaining to do, Annie—"

"I should think so," Tonia broke in.

"Come in here and sit down," he said, turning toward the living room. "At least the thieves left the furniture."

He and Annie ushered the thunderstruck pair to chairs, then sat together on the sofa facing them.

"Mother, why didn't you tell me?" Tonia demanded.

"I intended to this morning," Annie answered, glancing at Hank. "But I was so rattled when that awful, shrieking alarm went off...."

"Oops." Hank grimaced. "I forgot to warn you about that."

"That's all right, darling," Annie answered, clasping his hand. The two sat for an instant, staring into each other's eyes. Hank lifted her hand and rubbed it along his cheek.

Tonia watched her mother's face take on a melting wistfulness as she looked at Hank. Even reaching back into her dimmest childhood memories, she couldn't think of a time she had ever seen her mother look that way at anyone, even Tonia's father.

"Ahem." Ben cleared his throat, snapping them out of their fascination with each other.

"Oh, oh, where was I?" Annie said. "I tried to tell you. I *wanted* to, but when I got home, you were so distraught about Hank's theft and your disagreement with Ben, that I didn't have the heart to add to it. Also, I thought Hank and I should tell you together."

"Well," Ben breathed. "I'll be—"

"Benjamin!" his uncle warned.

"Fried! Why the big secret?"

"When did you meet?"

Ben and Tonia spoke at the same time, but Hank chose to answer her question first.

"On the cruise ship. Ben forced me to go on that vacation. I got to Puerto Vallarta all ready to go fishing but when I heard about this cruise ship coming through, I decided to hop aboard."

"This is beginning to sound like *The Love Boat*," Ben grumbled.

"Exactly!" His uncle beamed at him. "I met Annie there. It was love at first sight. It happened just that way with Maggie, too, forty-five years ago, in a London bomb shelter during the war." He and Annie happily went back to staring into each other's eyes.

"Why the subterfuge?" Ben demanded.

"Because of the Barbie dolls," his uncle answered, dragging his gaze from Annie's.

"The *what*!"

If she hadn't been so irritated with her mother and Hank, Tonia would have laughed at the murderous expression on Ben's face.

"Chloe, and before her, Catherine, and before her Marissa, or whatever her name was. All those long-legged, career-minded blondes you've dated for the past ten years. I knew you weren't going to marry any of them and since you've started expanding the business, it's taking up more and more of your time. I figured you wouldn't get around to marriage unless I helped you out."

"Well, of all the—"

"Let me finish, son, before you get all hot under the collar."

"I'm already hot under the collar!"

Hank gave Ben a stern look. Ben flipped his hand in an impatient gesture. "Go ahead."

"When I met Annie, she told me all about her daughter, and I told her all about you. We thought you two would be just right for each other—like we are."

Annie gave him another melting smile causing him to slide closer and slip his arm around her.

"It's a Gypsy mother's right to choose a mate for her child," she said.

"Oh, *Mamio*, how could you?" Tonia groaned. The situation between her and Ben, difficult before, was now hopelessly complicated. "I don't like being manipulated, and neither does Ben."

Annie looked sheepish. "We didn't see it that way. We thought if we just got you two together, nature would take its course."

"Which it did," Hank added.

The phone rang in the entryway. Lucy got it on the second ring, and they could hear her low voice speaking to the caller.

Ben stood and began pacing the room. "I knew there was something behind this book-writing scheme."

"I always wanted to do it," Hank defended. "When Annie told me Tonia was interested in doing one on the Gypsies but didn't know how to get started, I decided to go ahead with my book on Western lawmen. Annie suggested I call Dr. Justin to get a recommendation to cover my tracks."

"No wonder he didn't seem to know what I was talking about," Tonia declared, flouncing back against the chair cushions. "And I'll bet Mother told you about my claustrophobia."

"Well, now I understand why you were acting so crazy when you got back from Mexico," Ben said. "Practical jokes. Dyed hair."

Annie gave Hank's darker hair an admiring look.

"Elevator shoes," Tonia added.

"Your mother's my height. When she wears heels, she's taller."

"What were you saying about catching a tuna?" Tonia asked, remembering what they had been talking about in the hall.

"Hank came down for the weekend," Annie answered. "I had never been deep-sea fishing, so he took me. My first time."

Annie smiled at him. Hank's arm tightened around her.

Tonia was beginning to think her mother had probably had a lot of "firsts" with Hank.

"He was probably standing there listening when I called to tell you Ben had proposed."

From across the room, Ben's head whipped toward her.

"Yes," Annie smiled. "We had a wonderful celebration afterward."

"I'll bet," her daughter sniffed. Her gaze was snagged by Ben's startled look, and he lifted a questioning brow at her. She looked away.

"Uncle Hank—"

Seeing that Ben was ready to deliver a few scathing remarks, Hank raised his hand. "I know, son. I shouldn't have interfered. Everything would have worked out okay if..." his eyes went to the empty cases and the bare spots on the walls.

Immediately Ben looked contrite and walked over and laid a hand on his uncle's shoulder. "Yeah, Uncle Hank. I guess I understand, but I want to talk about this more, later." His fingers tightened briefly against the blue cloth of Hank's shirt, then he looked over at Tonia. "At least some of your books were saved, though."

Hank and Annie both sat up straight. "They were?"

"Yes, the ones that were at the bindery. Tonia picked them up and had them at her house."

Her heart pounding, Tonia stared at Ben, seeing Ben's statement for what it was. An apology and a request that they start again.

"Well, hot damn!" Hank crowed. "Two of those were the rarest ones in my collection."

A violent rattle of crockery drew their attention to the doorway. Lucy was holding a heavy coffee tray, but her hands were shaking so badly she looked close to dropping it.

Ben hurried across to take the tray from her. The whiteness of Lucy's face drew Tonia to her feet.

"Lucy, what's wrong?"

"I j-just got a call from Melvin." She sobbed. "He's leaving town."

The four in the room exchanged looks. While they were sorry her boyfriend was leaving, they hardly thought it was a crisis, considering what they had been through.

"Well, uh, that's too bad," Tonia began.

Lucy flicked an impatient look at her. "You don't understand. . . . I think *he* stole Hank's stuff!"

CHAPTER NINE

TONIA'S FIRST REACTION was to burst out laughing. "Melvin?"

"Yes. And—and I think George was involved, too."

"George?" Ben asked, frowning.

"Her brother. Remember, he was at Hank's party?"

Ben shot her a look. "And you were talking to him that night in Old Town."

Before Tonia could decipher his tone, he went on, "Why do you suspect them, Lucy?"

Lucy's startling announcement had brought Hank bounding up from the sofa. He hurried across the room to her, with Annie close behind.

"Yes, why?" Hank echoed.

Faced with so many questions and shocked expressions, Lucy almost dissolved into tears once more. She began digging in her pocket for a tissue.

Seeing that Ben was losing patience with the girl, Tonia laid a hand on her arm. "You've got to tell us what you suspect, Lucy, before it's too late."

Lucy nodded, dabbing at her eyes. "George was in prison. It was just for petty theft and writing bad checks. Nothing big like—like art theft. He got out a couple of months ago and promised he would straighten out his life. I was so happy when he got the job with Dr. Justin. He seemed to like working in the shop, even got jobs for Melvin...and me."

Her apologetic look wavered toward Hank, whose face was gray with anguish. "I'm sorry, Hank. I think George took my keys—remember the day I couldn't find them?—and had copies made. Melvin knows a little about electronics and stuff—his dad was an electrician—and when we were kids, Melvin used to work with him."

"Well," Ben breathed, his face thunderous. "I'll be damned. Why didn't you say something sooner?"

Lucy trembled. "I couldn't believe George was involved. After the bibliography disappeared, I asked him about it, but he got mad and said I always suspected him of things, and besides, what would he use it for? Melvin said he wasn't involved, either." She twisted the tissue in her fingers and gave Tonia a tearful look.

Tonia remembered the day she had come upon the tense scene in the kitchen. The two of them must have been arguing about it then.

"Did you give their names to the police, Ben?" Hank asked.

"I did," Tonia answered. "Along with everyone else's who was at the party. They probably haven't been questioned yet."

"I think it's time they answered a few questions," Ben declared. "Where did this Melvin call from just now?"

Lucy appeared to waver. Tonia sympathized with her loyalty to her brother and her desire to believe in his supposed reformation, but the girl had come too far to stop now. "Lucy, if they're involved, we have to know!"

Annie came over and slipped an arm around the girl's shoulders.

A ragged sigh rasped from Lucy's throat. "Melvin called from their boarding house. It's downtown. On Ash Street." She gave the address in a defeated tone of voice.

Ben spun toward the entryway, Tonia right behind him. "Aren't you going to call the police?" she asked.

He paused with his hand on the doorknob. "I will when I get there. Why call them for a false alarm, if these two have taken off? Besides, they'll have to get a search warrant, if I find anything."

"Then I'm coming with you."

"The hell you are!"

"The heck I'm not!"

"Hank . . . Mrs. Meier—can you do something with this stubborn woman?"

"Hank . . . Mom. Please stay out of this!"

They faced each other across the open doorway. The morning fog had cleared, leaving midmorning light to stream in upon them. The lines of Ben's face, always sharply angled, seemed grim. His night had been as rough as hers, she thought. As she watched, the coldness in his eyes softened, and he spoke gruffly.

"I don't want you to get hurt."

"I don't want *you* to get hurt. Besides, I have a right to prove my innocence."

He stared at her another moment. "You don't have to prove anything. I knew last night that you weren't involved. I was grasping at straws like a bullheaded jerk."

"I'll admit you were a jerk, but please let me go with you, anyway," she said. Her eyes held an apology for the things she had said the day before. There was no time now to tell him how she felt—she couldn't let him go without her.

Ben shook his head in defeat. "Why do I ever think I can get the better of you? All right, come on." He swung the door wide.

"Be careful," Hank called out, echoed by Annie.

"Don't worry, I'll watch her."

"That's not what they meant!" Tonia protested.

They dashed down the stairs. Ben swung open the car door for Tonia and rounded to his own side. The engine was started, and he was pulling away from the curb before she had slammed the door and buckled her seat belt.

The Jensen roared down the freeway, darting around traffic and traveling so fast Tonia was afraid to look at the speedometer. She was wondering if Ben had a secret ambition to be a race car driver, when he pulled off the freeway and slowed to take the access road that led to Ash Street. The neighborhood of Victorian homes that had been converted into offices and boarding houses was quiet. They located the address Lucy had given them and pulled up before a well-kept house.

"Why the disappointed look?" Ben asked, climbing from the low car.

"I thought it would look more like something from an old Edward G. Robinson movie," she answered, following him up the walk.

"Now who's jumping to conclusions?"

She made a face at him. "How are you going to get Melvin to talk to you?"

"He doesn't know me, so it shouldn't be a problem."

"He knows me, though."

"I don't suppose it would do me any good to ask you to stay in the car?"

"You guessed right on that one, partner."

Their knock was answered by an elderly woman in a neat pantsuit. Her makeup had been expertly applied, and she looked fresh from the hairdresser's.

Tonia, who had expected a slovenly woman with a cigarette dangling from her lips, could barely hide her surprise.

Ben jolted her by throwing his arm around her shoulders and facing the woman with a warm smile. "Good morning. Is Melvin here?"

"Melvin Morris?"

Ben hesitated and Tonia chimed in. "Yes. We'd like to see him."

"We're old friends of his from—"

"San Francisco," Tonia provided.

"We're only in town for a few days. On our honeymoon." Ben looked down at Tonia with a sappy smile.

Tonia stuck her hands behind her back, switched her birthstone ring from her right hand to her left, twisted it so it looked like a thin gold wedding band, then reached up to slip her hand through the bend in Ben's elbow.

The woman's eyes immediately went to the ring, and she answered Ben's charming smile with one of her own, obviously entranced with the sight of young love. "Melvin's in his room. I've heard a lot of activity up there." She gave them a conspiratorial wink. "I hope he's cleaning."

"Clearing is more like it," Ben murmured, and Tonia jabbed him in the ribs.

"He told us he'd found a nice place to live with a wonderful landlady," Ben went on. "Too bad he didn't mention how lovely you are. I'd have been here sooner. I'm embarrassed to admit I don't remember your name, though, Mrs...."

"Irving. Joyce Irving." The woman blushed prettily. "Won't you come in? I'll call Melvin down."

"No need," Ben said swiftly, stepping inside and dragging Tonia with him. "We'd like to surprise him."

The landlady agreed and looked as if she would swoon when Ben took her hand and placed a kiss on the back of it. "He's in the room at the top of the stairs, on the right," she breathed.

They left the woman standing in the hall and started up the stairs. "Laid it on a little thick, didn't you?" Tonia muttered.

"It's a dirty job, Tonia," he said solemnly. "But someone's got to do it."

She jabbed him in the ribs again.

At the top of the stairs, Ben turned toward the door that Mrs. Irving had indicated. Inside, they could hear movement.

Tonia pulled back on Ben's arm. "What are you going to say?"

"Whatever comes to mind in order to get in. Then I'll ask a lot of hard questions."

"Be careful."

He looked down at her with the warm, teasing light in his eyes that she hadn't seen in a couple of days. "Why Tonia, are you worried about me? I'm touched."

"Right now I would be worried about anyone," she said, suddenly flustered. "It could be dangerous."

"Uh-huh." He leaned over and kissed her cheek. "Thanks, honey. I love you, too."

He turned toward Melvin's door, leaving her with her mouth hanging open.

"Well—" she sputtered under her breath. "Now's a fine time to tell me!"

Ben, concentrating on what he would find behind Melvin's door, sent her a half grin. He lifted his hand and rapped on the wood. The sounds they had heard inside stopped.

He pounded the door again, a little louder.

"Who is it?" came a low request near the door.

"It's Ben," he answered loudly for the benefit of Mrs. Irving who was, no doubt, listening downstairs. "Open up. We came to see you."

"Ben who?"

"Ben Andrews." His voice lost its jovial tone, and he spoke low and clear. "You can either answer my questions now, or talk to the police in a few minutes."

The door was jerked open. Melvin stuck his head out. "I don't know anyone named Andrews." His eyes went past Ben to Tonia. "Oh, Miss Meier." His eyes popped, and his voice squeaked.

"Hello, Melvin. I think you'd better talk to us. Lucy says you are planning to leave town very suddenly."

Melvin stared at them a moment longer, his pale blue eyes wary. Finally, he opened the door and let them in.

The room's cheery country charm was belied by the mess Melvin had scattered around. Half-packed boxes were piled atop the bed, tilting crazily against each other. Two bulging suitcases waited by the door.

Now that she was facing him, Tonia wasn't as nervous as she thought she would be. "Melvin, Ben is Hank Tyson's nephew. We want to talk to you because we think you know about the burglary at Hank's house."

Melvin looked at the tall, hard-faced man before him. His Adam's apple bobbed. "I don't know anything."

Ben took a step closer and let the door shut behind him. "Don't add lying to your other crimes. Tell us what you know."

Melvin's sallow skin took on a fiery flush. "I don't know anything!"

Ben took another step. "You may be suffering a lapse of memory. Let me refresh it. You've been to Hank's house a number of times. You know he has a valuable art and book collection. You know it has disappeared, and now you're suddenly leaving town.... I met a couple of police officers yesterday who would be very interested in discussing this with you."

Melvin had pale eyebrows and lashes that made him look as if he was in a state of perpetual surprise. That innocent look couldn't disguise the shadow that passed over his face when he saw Ben's grim expression. "I didn't do it," he muttered.

Ben took another step toward him.

"I didn't! George made a duplicate key from one he took from Lucy. When he saw Tyson leave with Lucy and didn't see her wrecked-up old VW—" he nodded in Tonia's direction "—he thought the house was empty. He got inside, but you came in. When George knew you were both in the vault he shut the door."

Tonia gasped.

Sensing her reaction, Ben reached over and pulled her to him. His face was so hard it could have been carved in granite.

"Go on," he said.

A nervous tic began in Melvin's lips. "Then, uh, George, took that list of books and stuff that was on the desk. He said it was a lucky break for him, but I think Lucy let it slip that the old man was careless about things like that. Thought the burglar alarm and electronic locks could protect his stuff."

"How foolish of him to think he had a right to expect his things to be left alone," Ben observed in a voice that dripped venom. "What did he do with the list?"

Melvin's colorless lashes blinked. "Gave it to Dr. Justin, of course."

"Justin?"

"Whatever for!" Tonia burst out.

"To see which ones he could get a buyer for."

"A buyer?" Tonia said, uncomprehending.

Ben was several seconds ahead of her in decoding Melvin's meaning.

"You mean that professor you and George work for was behind all this?"

"That's ridiculous," Tonia scoffed. "I don't believe it! I've known Dr. Justin for years. He would never do something like this."

"It's true! That's why he hired us. He wanted someone with George's background."

"Prison record, you mean."

"Well, yeah. This was our first job for him. He's been working on his own for a long time."

Incensed, Tonia exclaimed, "You're a liar as well as a thief!"

"I've got news for you, miss. He's been doing this for months. He comes out smelling like a rose, and jerks like me take the rap. Well, I'm not sticking around to end up in jail."

Melvin made a sudden move toward the door, but Ben was there before him. He planted one of his square, powerful hands in the middle of Melvin's skinny chest.

"Wait a minute. Where are George and Justin now?"

Melvin's face screwed into a rebellious frown. Ben's hand slid up to make a garrote of the boy's open collar.

When he squeezed, Melvin squeaked out, "Hey, you're choking me!"

"Talk!"

"Otis is supposed to be making arrangements to get the stuff out of the country. George is at the shop."

"Shop?"

"You mean the one in Old Town?" Tonia asked.

"Yeah."

Ben let go of Melvin's collar and grabbed him around the shoulders, shoving him toward the door. "I'm going to call the police—then let's go for a little ride. You can finish your story on the way."

With Tonia close at their heels, Ben shoved Melvin out the door and hustled him down the stairs. They were brought up short at the sight of Mrs. Irving waiting downstairs. Her sweet face was puckered into a frown of concern.

"Everything all right, Melvin dear?"

The young man, who at the moment didn't look like he was anybody's "dear" anything, let out another squeak when Ben's grip tightened. What appeared as a friendly gesture from the front, was in fact a very painful warning.

"We're just going out for a while, ma'am," Tonia answered. "I've never seen Old Town, and Melvin has agreed to show us some of the more interesting sights. I wonder, though, if I could use your phone first?"

Mrs. Irving's benign smile collapsed into a frown. "Oh, dear, I'm afraid mine isn't working properly. Melvin, you were going to fix that for me," she scolded gently.

He gave her a sickly smile.

"He'll do it as soon as he gets back," Tonia assured her.

Mrs. Irving gave Melvin a grateful look and gestured them on their way. "Well, have fun. And, Melvin, try to stay out of the sun. Your face is quite red enough already."

Melvin's garbled answer was lost as Ben hurried him out the door.

They stuffed him into the tiny back seat of the Jensen, and Tonia got into the front, effectively blocking his escape.

After Ben had started the motor and pulled away from the curb, he lanced a hard look at his captive. "Okay, keep talking. What happened after George took the bibliography?"

Apparently deciding it was better to do as Ben said, Melvin took a deep breath and began. "Otis checked off the books he wanted—the ones he could get the most money for—and sent us back to make sure the old man really had them. Everyone was gone except Lucy. I kept her busy in the kitchen while George looked around. There was a bunch of books missing, the best ones, Otis said. He was pretty mad."

Ben growled. "Isn't that just too bad."

Melvin shot a worried look at the man driving the car and apparently decided he'd better finish his story. "So when Otis saw you two at Micaela's, he decided we should look in Tonia's house for the books. He thought she might be working with them at home."

Tonia's mind was reeling at the evidence of Dr. Justin's treachery. She remembered their meeting that night—his nervous excitement...his jokes about his "profitable business." She turned to Melvin, her eyes full of horror. "He sent you to break into my house?"

Melvin glanced out the window. "Yeah. Didn't do us any good 'cause we couldn't find them. And you almost caught us."

The hurt anger she had felt that night came flooding back. "Did you have to tear my house apart?" she demanded. To her that was the ultimate indignity.

"George said we had to make it look like kids had vandalized the place, since it wasn't a normal burglary."

His nonchalant answer infuriated Tonia, and she was preparing a scathing speech when Ben interrupted. "So you planned the burglary of Hank's house when you knew he would be out of town."

"I didn't do it!" Melvin insisted, sitting forward in the cramped space.

"Uh-huh."

"I didn't. You've got to believe me. I knew I was getting in deeper and deeper, but I didn't actually want to take anything. It seemed like fun at first—the way George talked."

Melvin ran his hands up and down his thighs. Watching him, Tonia remembered what she had read in his palm. Easily led, it had told her, wanting to impress people, willing to take the punishment meant for others. She had attached no special significance to this at the time. Now it was as if the character lines had been highlighted in red ink.

"I backed out," Melvin continued. "Told Otis and George I wasn't going along with it. I disappeared 'til this morning. Stayed with a friend until I knew George and Otis would be working on getting the shipment out, then I came to pack my stuff." He paused and added, "I shouldn't have called Lucy."

"Yeah," Ben agreed grimly. "You should have never stayed in her life or taken up with her brother after he got out of jail. Do you realize the police suspect her? They're taking her in for questioning this morning."

"She had nothing to do with it!" Melvin protested.

"You'll have to tell the police that."

Tonia gave Ben a puzzled look, wondering if Lucy was really a suspect. He may have made the story up to get Melvin to cooperate. If Melvin was vulnerable about anything besides his fears and a desire to save his own neck, it might be Lucy.

Busy with her own thoughts, Tonia barely noticed when they pulled into Old Town. Ben headed into a parking lot and began searching for a space.

Tonia sat up straight. "What are we going to do?"

"Call the police," Ben answered, swinging into an empty parking place. "We'll ask them to get a search warrant, although they could get in without one. I understand reasonable belief that stolen goods are on the premises would be enough to hold up in court. We'd better be legal about it, though. Come on, Melvin. You're going to help us get inside."

"No!" Melvin said, recoiling against the seat as if he'd taken a load of buckshot to the chest. His eyes rolled in his head, and his face paled even more. "George will kill me if he thinks I brought you here!"

Ben whipped around to face him. His hand shot out and once again grasped the wilted collar of Melvin's shirt. "You owe it to Lucy. You want her to go to jail?"

Melvin tried to stare Ben down, then with a half laugh of defiance, he shook his head.

They climbed from the car and Melvin led them to Dr. Justin's shop. From several yards away they could see it had a Closed sign on the door. Because it was at the end of a line of several shops, with an alley at the far side, few shoppers and sightseers strolled nearby.

Ben, with Melvin by his side, called the police from a booth and returned to where Tonia waited. "I talked to Detective Rios," Ben said, coming back to her side. "He said not to do anything foolish until he gets here, so I want you to stay out here."

Her hands lifted to her hips. "While you do what?"

"Talk to George, if he's in there, of course. There's a chance they already got Hank's stuff out of the country."

"Rios probably meant for neither of us to do anything foolish, but if you're going in there, I am, too."

Ben's breath hissed out as he cursed under his breath. "Tonia, this is no time to argue!"

"No, it isn't." She turned to go. "Are you coming?"

"We're going to have a talk about this later, woman," he grumbled.

"I can't wait. Melvin, do you have a key?" She looked back over her shoulder to see that Melvin had started to slip away while she and Ben were arguing.

"Going somewhere, Melvin?" Ben asked, stepping up behind him.

"No," he muttered with a resigned sigh. "I think I can get George to open up for me."

"Wait a minute—" Tonia placed a hand on Ben's arm. "I have an idea that might work better."

She spoke quickly in a low voice. It took her several moments to convince him her plan was good.

At the door she motioned the two men to stand back, and rapped softly on the glass.

Tonia was nervous. She felt as if a thousand butterflies were beating themselves to death against the walls of her stomach.

Apprehension in her eyes, she looked across at Ben on the opposite side of the door. He had positioned himself out of sight so that Tonia would be the only one George saw when he opened the door. Melvin was behind Ben and looked prepared to jump out of the way at the first sign of trouble.

Ben's face was hard, his eyes watchful. "Remember," he mouthed at her. "You're a good actress, and he's just a *gaje*."

She gave him a shaky smile.

"The shop's closed!" George bellowed from inside.

Tonia rapped softly on the glass again. "George, open up."

She heard a scuffling sound inside, then a voice close to the door. "Who's there?"

"Antonia Meier. Open the door. I want to talk to you."

Several dead bolts were turned, and the door opened. One suspicious brown eye peered out at her through the crack allowed by the chain lock. "What do you want? Dr. Justin isn't here."

"I don't want to see him. I want to see you."

The crack widened a fraction of an inch. "Oh, yeah?"

Tonia forced a smile. "Yeah."

"What about?"

"I thought maybe we could get together," she said, giving him what she hoped was a seductive smile. "Maybe do some business."

Through the tiny crack he allowed himself, Tonia could see he was unshaven and wearing a tight, dirty T-shirt. His gaze roamed over her, taking in the loose red blouse and snug slacks she wore. He smirked. "Get together, huh? Yeah, I noticed you watching me at that party the old dude had, and that night you were down here for dinner."

Tonia nearly gagged as she forced out the lie. "Yes, I was. Now I want a cut of what you took from my boss."

The sly grin vanished from George's face. "I don't know what you're talking about."

"Sure you do. I saw you checking out Hank's things that night. I knew who had burglarized his place as soon as I talked to the police." She watched his face, refusing to let her eyes slide sideways to Ben's.

"I ain't doin' no deal. This is already split too many ways."

"I think you'd better...."

He considered her for a moment, his eyes drifting around the square. As a group of tourists carrying big packages and expensive cameras passed into view, he seemed to make a sudden decision. "All right—come on. We'll talk."

The door closed all the way and when the chain rattled off its track, Tonia could feel Ben beside her, tensing for action.

The instant George opened the door, Ben was inside. In a flash he had pushed the other man up against a display counter.

"What the—" George sputtered, fighting to regain the initiative from Ben.

"Just shut up," Ben growled, grabbing George's arm and spinning him around.

Tonia rushed in after them and swung back to shut the door. Disgusted but unsurprised, she saw that Melvin had disappeared.

"All right, where's my uncle's stuff?"

George didn't answer but threw a malevolent look over his shoulder in Ben's direction.

Tonia's eyes darted around and came to rest on a storeroom door that yawned open at the back of the shop. She could see some of Hank's valuables jumbled together in a pile in the center of the room's floor. The sight infuriated her, reminding her of her own ransacked house. She darted forward.

"There, Ben."

"Tonia, wait. Don't go in there." Ben came after her, dragging George with him.

She only half heard him, her eyes intent on Hank's priceless Remington bronze, lying on its side on the concrete floor. She bent to pick it up but froze when she heard the sounds of a scuffle behind her.

Before she realized what was happening or that she was the cause of it, Ben was catapulted inside, and the door was slammed shut behind him.

CHAPTER TEN

"OH, NO!"

"Well put," Ben spoke through the darkness, panting from his scuffle with George. He cursed under his breath, lifted his fist to pound on the door, then thought better of it. "You know, honey, you really can complicate things sometimes."

"I'm sorry, Ben. I didn't think.... I looked in here...saw Hank's things...and—oh, it's so dark and tiny in here," her voice trailed off as she gasped for air.

Ben groped toward her in the darkness, enfolding her in his arms. "Calm down. It'll be all right," he soothed, rubbing her shoulders lightly. "You can't fall apart now."

Tonia knew he was right. She drew in several deep, calming breaths. "I'll be okay."

"Good girl," he said, turning her slowly around with him as he studied their prison. "Well, Miss Impetuous, we've got to figure out how to get out of here."

"Is this what Detective Rios meant by doing something foolish?" she asked against his chest.

"Yeah. But I think I've found a way for us to redeem ourselves. Or at least get ourselves out."

She looked up to discover that her eyes were adjusting to the darkness.

This wasn't the Cimmerian blackness the vault had been. A bit of illumination was coming from somewhere.

Ben was leaning back, looking up at the old-fashioned high ceiling. "If I don't miss my guess, that's a painted-over skylight," he said, pointing to a ghostly square over their heads. "You're going to have to go up there and open it."

"Me!"

"Well, *I* can't squeeze through it. We've got to get out of here before George comes back. There's no telling what he might do when he realizes he left the merchandise in here with the captives."

"But—"

"You're not afraid of heights, too, are you?"

"Certainly not."

"It'll have to be you. Did you see a table in here? Or a chair?"

"No. Just Hank's things jumbled all over the floor. His Remington bronze is right over there," she said gesturing toward the dark shape across the room. "You'd think it was something they had picked up at the swap meet. I'm beginning to think this is some rinky-dink burglary ring if they can't take any better care of their merchandise than that."

"Be grateful," Ben grunted, pulling her with him as he felt his way around the room.

They came to a door that appeared to be unlocked but wouldn't budge. Ben rattled the knob and pushed his shoulder against it. "If they'd known what they were doing, the stuff would have been out of the country within minutes of the theft. Although maybe some of the merchandise has already gone out. I didn't notice any boxes of books, did you?"

"No."

"They may have shipped those already or have them stashed somewhere else. I'm wondering if this didn't just start out as an adventure for Justin. Now he's not sure what to do."

"Maybe. What are you looking for?" she finally asked on their third circuit of the room.

"Something for you to stand on. There's nothing, so it'll have to be my shoulders."

"What?" she squeaked, pulling away.

"There's no other way. I don't suppose you were on the high school gymnastics team, were you?"

"Swimming."

"I'd hoped you would know how they climb up on each other. I guess we'll have to work freestyle."

"Great."

"Don't sound so glum," he commanded. "I'll be doing most of the work. You only have to climb out and through the skylight."

"Only!"

"Come on. Here, put your hand on my shoulder and your foot right—what kind of shoes are those? Sandals? You'll have to take them off."

Tonia did as she was told, slipping her sandals off and leaving them in the center of the room. She knew her bare feet would be easier on Ben, if she did manage to stand up on his shoulders. Scrambling out onto the roof with no shoes would be a different matter—if she got to the roof.

"All right," she said, her voice shaking. "I'm ready."

Ben grasped her shoulders and pulled her to him. "Tonia, you're our only way out. You can do this." For an instant his mouth fused with hers, and she wanted to melt into him, burrowing against his chest to hide from what she had to do.

Pressing a kiss to her hair, he eased her away from him, placed her hands on his shoulders and his around her waist. "Now, put your foot on my thigh." He bent his knee to form a shelf for her to stand on. She did as he said, springing off her other foot and twisting around.

She overshot her mark, but Ben tried to compensate by throwing his weight in the other direction, and they ended in a heap on the floor.

They froze, listening. Several long seconds ticked by.

"Ben, do you think—"

"Hush, our friend George probably heard that and will be in here with a baseball bat."

"Maybe we could overpower him," she whispered. "You know, stand behind the door when he opens it and—"

"Tonia," he groaned. "This isn't *Mission Impossible*."

"It was only a suggestion. You don't have to get huffy. I think," she went on, trying to push Ben's bulk off her left leg, "this business of climbing onto your shoulders is going to take some practice."

"No kidding," Ben answered, maneuvering her right foot out of the pit of his stomach. "I don't think George heard us or he would be in here by now. Come on, let's try it again."

They managed to make it to their feet, and once again Ben formed a stepping place for her with his knee. This time he placed his hands firmly about her waist at just the right instant, giving her leverage. He let go in time to let her slither around to place her bare feet at his waist and climb up his back like a monkey.

In a few seconds she was seated on his shoulders.

Tonia gasped in surprise, not quite sure how it had come about. She clutched at Ben's head.

"Don't pull my hair out," he said. When her grip loosened, he settled her more firmly with his hands on her knees. "Now stand up on one foot and then the other. I'll hold your ankles."

"I don't suppose we could do this against a wall?"

He grunted at her plaintive tone. "No, then I'd have to walk across the room with you standing on my shoulders. You want that?"

"No!"

"Well hurry up, then. You're a lot heavier than you look."

She jerked his hair, took a deep breath for courage, then leaned to one side and lifted her right foot to his shoulder. Balancing herself against his head, she rose slowly, her breath coming in little puffs. Once she almost overbalanced, and Ben scrambled to grab her ankles. Righting herself, she found she was standing on his shoulders, able to reach the skylight easily.

"Is it locked?"

"Yes. Rusted, too, I think."

Tonia gripped the skylight frame with one hand and the lock with the other. She began to twist the small bolt from side to side, loosening years of rust. Several years worth of dust rained down in her face.

She stopped to wipe her eyes, and returned to her task.

Within moments her arms ached from exertion. She kept at it though, working the bolt back and forth until it squeaked loudly and slid free.

"I did it!"

"Good girl! Now see if you can push it open and climb out. Then find out where George is, and see if you can either let me out, or call Rios from that pay phone."

"I'll call Rios and see if he's on his way. Then I'll be back to let you out."

"Okay."

"Uh, Ben?"

"Yeah."

"I left my purse in the car."

"Oh, lord." Ben let go of one ankle, leaving her to scramble for a handhold on the skylight sill. She heard the jingle of change and then felt his fist knocking against her thigh.

She reached down and took the money from him, dropping it into her own pocket. "Thanks. I'm climbing out now." In a moment she had shoved the skylight open. She heaved herself up and off Ben's shoulders, blinking against the sunlight, and turned to look down at Ben who was watching her.

Head tilted back, hands on hips, his face looked worried. "Be careful. Melvin's around somewhere, too, you know. He disappeared when George opened the shop door, but I don't think he went far. Try to be quiet as you climb down off the roof. I'll make a lot of racket in here."

Tonia nodded and turned to look around. A maintenance ladder curved up and over the edge of the flat roof.

"There's a ladder," she whispered down to him. "I'll be around to let you out in just a minute."

"Be careful," Ben said once again as she stood and crept away from the skylight. Below her, she heard Ben beating on the door and demanding to be released. His shouts covered any noise she made.

The roof was the graveled kind, with little white rocks that sparkled in the sun—and were murder on Tonia's feet. She squinted her eyes against the glare coming off the roof, and scurried toward the ladder, keeping low and flinching at every step.

As soon as she reached the ladder, she could see that it led down to the back of the shop on the alley. The alley itself was bordered by a security fence lined with overgrown oleander bushes. On the other side was a nearly deserted parking lot.

She sighed. Not only was there no cop around when she needed one. There was no one at all.

Cautiously, she pulled herself to the edge of the ladder and looked straight down. She could see that the steps ended beside the door to the room where Ben was trapped. She and Ben hadn't been able to open the door because a small white panel van was backed up against it. The van's side door was open, and she realized that George had probably been loading merchandise into it before she and Ben showed up.

She waited several moments to see if he would return. When he didn't, she scrambled down the ladder and hurried around to the van's open door.

Inside were several unmarked cardboard boxes. She gave one a push. When it hardly moved, she decided the sealed cartons were filled with Hank's books.

Her lips tightened in anger. They weren't going to get away with this. Turning, she started away from the back of the shop, rounded the corner and came face-to-face with Melvin.

And George.

"How did you get out?" Melvin asked, bug-eyed.

"Oh, great," George snapped. "Grab her."

Tonia whirled to run in the other direction. She banged her bare toes against a jutting piece of concrete, stumbled and almost fell. Before she could regain her balance, George was on her. He gripped her around the waist with one arm and clamped his other hand over her mouth.

She struggled, trying to whip her head away while clawing at his hands, face, whatever she could reach. His hand over her mouth was cutting off her air, but she still struggled.

The fear she had felt earlier was burned away in a moment of raw fury. This was the man who had vandalized her home. He could have entered, looked for what he wanted and left her things intact. Instead, he had ripped his way through her house because he'd *wanted* to.

She fought him, twisting her lesser weight to keep him off balance, while clutching, scratching and pinching at his hands and arms.

"Damn it, settle down!" George demanded savagely. "Or something real unpleasant's going to happen to you and your boyfriend."

He was furious—and desperate. Tonia wasn't sure what he might do to her and Ben. With a last defiant jerk, she quieted, allowing her body to go limp until she could form another plan.

"I'll get her back inside," George said to Melvin, who had watched the whole struggle in silence. "But I'll have to stay and watch her. You finish loading the truck."

"Me?" Melvin whined. "I wasn't even in on this deal. I want to go."

"Do as you're told," George snapped. "You brought 'em here, and you're gonna pay for it."

Although she knew he was at the end of his patience and desperate, Tonia struggled again and managed to free her mouth.

"Don't do it, Melvin. You don't have to do his dirty work for him."

"You shut up," George snarled. He started to put his hand over her mouth again, but Melvin grabbed his arm.

"Melvin—I read your palm—I know you," she said urgently, while his pale eyes fixed on her and his face worked with emotion. "You want people to like you. But people use you. George uses you. Has all your life."

Melvin's pale eyes darted from her to George, uncertainty in his face. "You said nobody would get hurt, George. You said the old man could afford it because he was rich and the stuff was insured. You didn't tell me the cops would think Lucy did it."

"They don't think that," his partner scoffed. "She's just a kid."

Ben's gamble had paid off, Tonia thought frantically. Melvin believed Lucy was in jeopardy. George didn't care if she was or not.

Tonia pushed her advantage. "She could go to jail. The police think she's an accomplice."

"Don't listen to her," George demanded, trying to free his arm from Melvin's grasp. "She's just gaffing."

To her amazement, Tonia watched the uncertainty melt from Melvin's eyes to be replaced with fury.

"You don't care!" Melvin shouted. "She's your own sister—and you don't care what happens to her."

He jerked George's arm free from Tonia and took a swing at him.

In a flash Tonia scampered away. Ignoring any pain to her bare feet, she rushed to the front of the shop. George had left the door closed, but it was unlocked, so she whipped it open and ran to free Ben who was still bellowing to be let out. She jerked the door open and tumbled into his arms.

"Tonia, are you all right? What took so long? Did you call Rios? Where's George?"

"He and Melvin are slugging it out in the alley behind the shop."

"Good lord, woman, what have you been doing?" Ben didn't wait for an answer but grabbed her, shoved her sandals into her hand and ran through the shop.

Tonia hopped behind him, trying to slide her sandals on and keep up with him at the same time.

When she emerged from the shop, she saw Ben and Melvin holding George, who was still cursing and struggling. Two police cars were just pulling into the parking lot, followed by two television news teams.

THE IMAGE OF THE ARREST faded from the screen to be replaced by the anchorman's serious face as he repeated the information that a university professor had been caught at the San Ysidro border crossing. He had been carrying several thousand dollars and was suspected of dealing in stolen art and artifacts.

Ben stood up and switched off the television in Hank's living room.

They had spent hours with the police and were now settling down to go over the day's events. Detective Rios had given Ben and Tonia a speech about their foolishness and then thanked them for their help. He had promised that Hank's valuables would be returned in a few days but might be subpoenaed as evidence for the trial.

"Pretty good news report," Hank commented. He and Annie were seated on the sofa, holding hands.

"Yeah," Ben replied solemnly. "Especially that shot of Tonia looking like she had single-handedly captured public enemy number one."

Tonia sent him an arch look. "Well, somebody had to do it. You were busy lounging around in that storeroom."

"Lounging around!" Ben stalked over to her chair, looming over her in a threatening way. "You sure took your sweet time getting back to me."

Hank interrupted. "I can't believe I was such an old fool. I was so flattered when Justin wanted to know about my collection—I practically handed him the keys to the house! Told him which things were the most valuable...."

Ben swung back to his uncle. "Don't blame yourself, Uncle Hank. You were in the hands of a master. He'd been doing this for months. Taking small artifacts, mostly Indian and South American art and selling them. Detective Rios says he had a neat little operation going until he got greedy. And, of course, George and Melvin were too inept to do what he wanted them to do.''

The police told him that all three men would be charged, but that Melvin might be given a lighter sentence if he gave evidence against the other two. Ben suggested George would be glad to give evidence against Dr. Justin, also.

"I feel so bad about my part in it," Annie sighed. "When Hank and I cooked up this matchmaking scheme, I knew Tonia respected Dr. Justin so much that she would act on his recommendation to take a job without question." She gave Hank a melting glance. "And I knew she would like you right away and want the job." A look of consternation crossed her face. "I never expected..."

Hank drew her close. "Don't worry about it, honey. We were naive, but Justin was a thief." He stood up, pulling her with him. "Come on. Let's go see if we can help Lucy fix something to eat. She feels so bad about all this—as if it was her fault—and needs to keep busy, but if I drink any more of her coffee, I'll be awake for a month."

"Mmm," Annie said, leaning over to kiss him. "That sounds promising."

Tonia watched them leave the room, still amazed to see her mother being hugged and kissed by *her* boss.

Ben stood up from her chair and walked over to the windows that looked out over the Pacific. He stuck his hands in the back pockets of his jeans and rocked back on his heels. His hands came up to twirl the drapery cord. After a few moments, he dropped it and ran his hand around the back of his neck.

In any other man, Tonia would have taken his fidgeting as a sign of nervousness. But Ben Andrews didn't show nervousness in that way.

Even as the thought passed through her mind, he started patting his shirt pocket for his glasses.

"What do you think Lucy will do?" he finally asked, slipping the glasses onto his nose and turning his head to study her through the lenses.

"I don't know. She feels so guilty. She's going to find a lawyer for her brother. Poor girl, she'll probably stand by him and Melvin, although she's too good for either one of them."

"It might be better if she found a new job. Something more challenging than keeping house for Hank. Besides, your mom might want to hire her own household staff."

Tonia smiled. Her mother's "household staff" had always consisted of herself and Tonia.

"Maybe I can find her something in one of my stores. She might like it."

"Perhaps," Tonia offered into the next awkward silence that fell.

"Some day we've had, huh?" he said after several moments of painful quiet.

"Yes. Wild."

"You surprised me."

"I did?"

"When we were locked in that storeroom, you forgot all about your claustrophobia, and did what needed to be done."

She waited, not sure what answer he expected.

"Funny," he said, rubbing the back of his neck again. "I keep misjudging you."

"Ben...."

He held his hand up. "I know, I know. You're not surprised. You saw it in my palm." His face twisted with anguish. "Tonia...I'm sorry for what I said."

His pain hit her like a blow. "You already apologized."

"I didn't mean it, though."

"What?"

"Suspecting you was one way to keep from admitting I loved you."

Tonia's mouth opened, but no words came out.

"All those reasons I gave for marriage were so much bull. There was really only one." Ben sighed. "One way or another, I've been one heck of a fool."

"I was, too," she answered in a small voice. "I was unforgiving. I think I was scared and looking for an excuse to push you away."

His head jerked up, his gray eyes pinning her as he moved closer. "Why?"

She shrugged, reaching down to trail her fingers along the brown velvet of the chair, leaving twin tracks. "I guess after my experience with Greg, I wasn't sure of my feelings. I keep expecting you to have no flaws."

"You know all my flaws. You know me better than anyone does," he said.

He walked to her chair and held out his hand. She stared at it for an instant.

This was the moment when they started again with no suspicions between them or manipulations from anyone else. Ben stared at her, compelling her to accept his hand—accept him.

Slowly, Tonia's own hand lifted to slide across his well-remembered palm.

He drew her to her feet. "And I know you...and love you," he continued. "Are you ready to accept my proposal?"

She nodded, smiling into his face. "I love you, too."

"Thank God," Ben breathed, lowering his head to kiss her. "I thought you'd never admit it."

Her breath puffed out in a laugh as his lips touched hers. "I thought *you* would never admit it!"

His kiss was long, offering the reassurance they both needed. Tonia reveled in it.

Ben drew away, gazing down at her with eyes silvered with promise and desire. "When can we get married?"

"Whenever you say."

"Are you always going to be this agreeable?"

"No."

They laughed as their lips touched again, and within moments, they were lost to their surroundings....

"WELL, ANNIE, I guess we're pretty good matchmakers, after all." Hank's gleeful voice drifted in from the doorway.

The couple by the window ignored him.

"You were right," Annie agreed dreamily, hugging him. "Do you think we should start planning a *double* Gypsy wedding?"

"Sounds good. We'll have it soon." He kissed her, then drew back, a devilish twinkle in his eyes. "How long do you think it will be before those two get some news from the stork?"

ATTRACTIVE, SPACE SAVING BOOK RACK

Display your most prized novels on this handsome and sturdy book rack. The hand-rubbed walnut finish will blend into your library decor with quiet elegance, providing a practical organizer for your favorite hard-or soft-covered books.

Only $9.95

Approximately 16" x 8" when assembled

Assembles in seconds!

To order, rush your name, address and zip code, along with a check or money order for $10.70* ($9.95 plus 75¢ postage and handling) payable to *Harlequin Reader Service*:

Harlequin Reader Service
Book Rack Offer
901 Fuhrmann Blvd.
P.O. Box 1396
Buffalo, NY 14269-1396

Offer not available in Canada.

BKR-1A

*New York and Iowa residents add appropriate sales tax.

Harlequin American Romance

**Romances that go one step farther...
American Romance**

Realistic stories involving people you can relate to and
care about.

Compelling relationships between the mature men and
women of today's world.

Romances that capture the core of genuine emotions
between a man and a woman.

Join us each month for four new titles wherever paperback
books are sold.
Enter the world of American Romance.

Amro-1

**In the spellbinding tradition
of Barbara Taylor Bradford, a novel of
passion, destiny and endless love.**

_Season of
Loving_

Shirley Larson

He possessed everything: wealth, power, privilege—everything except the woman he desired and the son he loved more than life itself.

Available in February at your favorite retail outlet, or reserve your copy for January shipping by sending your name, address, zip or postal code, along with a check for $4.70 (includes 75¢ for postage and handling) payable to Worldwide Library to:

In the U.S.	In Canada
Worldwide Library	Worldwide Library
901 Fuhrmann Boulevard	P.O. Box 609
Box 1325	Fort Erie, Ontario
Buffalo, NY 14269-1325	L2A 5X3

Please specify book title with your order.

 **WORLDWIDE LIBRARY®**

SEA-1

◆ Harlequin Superromance

**Here are the longer, more involving stories you
have been waiting for...Superromance.**

Modern, believable novels of love, full of the complex
joys and heartaches of real people.

Intriguing conflicts based on today's constantly
changing life-styles.

Four new titles every month.
Available wherever paperbacks are sold.

SUPER-1
